ExUs

A Novel of the Future

By Josephus IV

ISBN-13: 978-1503034044

ISBN-10: 1503034046

Published by Josephus Publishing through CreateSpace. Contact: josephuspublishing@outlook.com

Second Edition, 2015

For Miss Sunshine, who started me thinking on these things.

Author Note

Many will attack this book as outrageous or worse. They will ask how I could suggest any possibility that these things might happen. They will say that simply discussing such ideas is highly destructive.

The point is to awaken you - so that nothing like this can ever happen in America. Please do not let this happen.

"The tyranny of virtue is worse than the tyranny of vice because virtue has no conscience." – Unknown

***

"For not just one alone has risen against us to destroy us, but in every generation they rise against us to destroy us, and the Holy One, blessed be He, saves us from their hand!" – Passover Haggadah

***

"A secret of tyranny is to persuade you that words like 'liberty', 'freedom,' 'equality', and 'justice' mean the opposite of their plain meaning." - Josephus IV

1

A few people still call me the "un-Mohel," although you may know my real name from the histories. If you want to know the meaning of that strange name, however, or if you know my real name and want to learn the truth, listen to this story.

Looking back now, from a small house in a faraway land, it all seems a dream. Yet I did help thousands of Jews – in fact, more than thousands - in a time of great trouble, which is how I earned that strange name. And, of course, the American Diaspora is no dream.

In 2017, when these events began, I was a geeky senior at Stuyvesant High School in New York City. I was just another generic late teen of the MultiFace generation – five eleven, skinny, rimless glasses, light brown hair, nondescript. I usually wore the same jeans, faded Giants t-shirt, and old sneakers. You would not have looked at me passing on the street. I was like a Chagall fiddler who had not yet learned the tune; I was not even on a roof.

My family was a usual unusual New York family. My mother, who had dreamt of singing on Broadway, taught math at an East Side public school.

My father, a lawyer in the City's Law Department, loved Japanese art and hiking the City's parks. We were a close family; we had dinner and quarreled together at least twice a week.

My parents were passionate about education. They, and their parents before them, saw education as the gateway to the greater world. Because New York private schools were beyond my parents' reach and ideology, I always attended public school. Yet they started me in math coaching when I was three - and music lessons at six.

It was a great investment. The music did not stick, unfortunately, but the math did. Math became my second language, a running white-board exercise in my brain. By age six I had mastered algebra and geometry.

Math and computers. I can't remember a time without tablets, tab-phones, and optical internet. From first grade on my comp-pad was an extension of my hand.

I can't remember a time when you could not see any movie, or start a new book, or hear any song, in longer than the nano-second it took to touch the right App.

There was never a time, also, when I did not have instant access, via that comp-pad, to the world's great math problems and the thoughts of the greatest mathematicians.

In school I was neither a leader nor loner. I had a few friends, with whom I had been thrown together first week of freshman year; we hung out and did math problems and computer stuff in free periods and after school. All were smart. Being at Stuy, we said, was a state of mind. We had the hubris of the young, untarnished by experience.

I got perfect grades. I was on the school math team (the only Jew – all the rest were Asians). I liked girls but did not have time for a girl.

I had two focus points – computer hacking and getting into Harvard.

Unknown to the School (probably the School didn't want to know), students competed each year for the best computer hack. Stuy students did not do drugs (maybe just a few); instead, to be cool, we hacked computers.

The hacking contest, called the "Hack", was a big deal. It had only three rules - one, no messing with Stuyvesant systems; two, do no harm; and three (of course), don't get caught.

What was the best hack? There were no precise metrics - but we knew the best when we saw it. Each year three seniors, the "Lords of Hack", were elected to judge the competition. They were recognized stars who had placed high in earlier years.

Freshman year, needless to say, as soon as I learned of the Hack, I entered. I worked very hard at that hack; then, when I failed to place, I was stunned. It was a jug of cold water in my face! Maybe there were indeed a few other smart people in this school!

Angry and embarrassed, I tried again sophomore year. I did not work any harder, but this time placed third!

Finishing high was a big deal, a very big deal. It restored my confidence. Now a lot of people at Stuyvesant knew who I was.

And then, junior year, I came in second!

My sophomore hack cracked the shopping cart programs of Amazon.com. It took only three weeks. I arranged to ship for free a separate title in fiction, science, economics, and history to each of the Lords of Hack. They really liked it.

Some of my competitors jeered that hacking Amazon was dull and boring; but the Lords gave me third place.

My junior-year hack was more daring. I took on a bank. In itself this was no big deal. Most banks had the same security firewalls. Even so, despite spending millions on security upgrades, they could not outpace the best hackers.

A small group of hackers always kept ahead. Some did it just to show they were smarter than the banks. Others hacked for money - to sell information or divert funds, and they made a pile! But the very best left no footsteps; no one knew they had been there - except occasionally the banks. The banks sometimes figured out they had been hacked but rarely - very rarely -identified a victim for indictment.

If you were good, however, you would never get caught.

Stealing money from banks, however easy, was bad juju. It was also uncool in our culture. (Like other tribes, we had our own code of honor, our "hackido".) In our tribe, also, if you hacked a bank, you had better be clever - you had to do something the Lords of Hack would think funny or cool.

My junior bank hack was <u>more than</u> funny or cool. I arranged for two banks to hack each other.

I made the first bank send to the second bank its files of officer compensation; and I made the second send to the first its monthly list of major commercial loans being submitted to its Credit Committee for review.

There was hell to pay at both banks; but the story never hit the press. The whole hack took only four weeks, with a great prize at the end.

For placing second I got a new super comp-pad with more power than a million of the computers that first sent a man to the moon. (To enter the competition you had to kick in $50; these fees paid for the three annual prizes.)

How to top that senior year?

Senior year - 2017, when this story begins – because I had placed second, my friends wanted me to run for election as a Lord of Hack. But, since being a Lord would mean I could not enter the comp, and since I did not really want to waste time judging, I stalled.

I told my friends I would think about it. The election was not until October; so I had time. I wanted to spend my free hours thinking up the ultimate first place hack.

Then, in the second week of school, while I was starting to plan out my hack, the School's college counselors called a senior class meeting.

The meeting was at ten o'clock on a bright October day (I always remember the time of day of important events in my life). It was in the main auditorium, meaning it was serious.

The five counselors for our class of 936 sat uncomfortably on the stage in the auditorium. The reason for their pain soon became clear.

The chief counselor, Mr. Schwartz, went to the lectern and called for quiet. He was a small, round man with glasses and a rumpled brown sport coat. He banged twice on the lectern to stop the talking and texting. When he got our attention, he cleared his throat. He had, he said, "unwelcome" news. That really got our attention.

Sitting at the side of the stage, the Teachers Union monitor made notes. She was a horrid looking woman in her fifties. Her job was to report "InAp Speech" by faculty or students (InAp - meaning "inappropriate" – that is, racist, sexist, homophobic or otherwise "unjust" conversation).

The penalty for any recorded "InAp Speech" was to be listed on the "Inappropriate Speech List" on the school's website, the duration of the listing being equal to the gravity of the offense.

Mr. Schwartz was very unhappy with his task. "How many of you know about the Victims Law?" he asked.

A scattering of hands went up. I knew vaguely that something called the Victims Law had passed Congress in the spring. I remembered my parents discussing it a lot; I had no interest in politics and paid little attention. Nothing could distract me from math and my computers.

"The Victims Law," said Mr. Schwartz, "or the 'V-Law' as it is called (he stressed the "V"), has changed the way college applications will be handled." He cleared his throat again.

"The law creates preferences for racial and ethnic groups - and for gender and sexual orientation." Mr. Schwartz was really uncomfortable. He looked over at the TU Monitor, worried what she might write. (Teachers could also be included on the InAp List. For a teacher such a listing could mean not just public opprobrium but pay deductions.)

"So, if you are African-American or Hispanic, or if you are a woman or gay, you now get first preference in college admissions. And, of course, in other things."

There was now dead silence.

Then someone shouted, "Suppose you are half black and half white?" Despite the threat of In-Ap listing, we were never inhibited in meetings with faculty (especially if the TU Monitor, on the stage, could not see who was speaking).

"They are publishing regulations," said Mr. Schwartz, "the Department of Health and Human Services. I think the regulations will have ways to determine who you are – er, what category you fit in."

"You mean, if we don't know whether we're black or gay!" someone shouted, causing a ripple of laughter around the auditorium.

The TU Monitor grimaced and made a note.

"I think there will be credits or preferences, or something like that, depending on the percentage of your ancestry," Mr. Schwartz said. "But we don't really know. It will be in the regulations."

The auditorium was again dead silent.

Mr. Schwartz straightened his tie. "What is important is this - now, under the V Law, the federal government will review all college applications. There will be two forms of application – one for Victims – that's what they call people who get these preferences – and the second for non-Victims. When you meet with your college counselor, they will take you through your application form."

"Does this mean that straight, white guys get pushed back?" someone shouted.

Now Mr. Schwartz was really uncomfortable.

"It means that colleges must give percentage preference to Victims in each Victim category," he said. It was the safest, most euphemistic answer he could think of.

"But white guys are not Victims, right?" shouted the same student.

Mr. Schwartz tugged at his tie. "Correct," he said. "White guys are not Victims."

"So white guys don't get any preference percentage, or whatever they call it, right?

"That is correct," said Mr. Schwartz.

"So white guys go to the back of the line!" shouted the student. He was proud of his syllogism.

"It is a correct inference, yes," said Mr. Schwartz, "that people who are not Victims will be placed after all Victim preferences have been satisfied." That was simply a statement of fact.

It was a now-silent senior class that filed out of the auditorium. There was no joking or kidding around. Each of us wondered what the Victims Law meant for us.

The Spectator, Stuyvesant's school newspaper, criticized Mr. Schwartz and the college counselors for a racist presentation. The editorial writer said that the discussion "dripped with white condescension". The writer was outraged, also, at the gibes from the audience, which were "grossly racist." He called for students to out the offenders so they could be published on the InAp Speech List.

2

The next week I met with my college counselor, who just happened to be Mr. Schwartz.

He started by asking if I had attended the meeting in the auditorium. I said I had. He said the School was requiring all the college counselors to apologize for the racism of the presentation. He hoped that I had not been offended. He said that his name had been put on the InAp Speech List for the tone of his comments, not the specifics (although he hastened to add that he had not received any payroll deduction).

I said I had not been offended.

"O.K.," he said. "Here's your application form. Let's go through it."

He handed me a five-page document printed on blue paper. At the top it stated: "Uniform College Application Form – Non-Victim".

After the senior class meeting in the auditorium, I had read everything I could about the Victims Law. For white males, it was pretty grim.

I went right to the point with Mr. Schwartz. "So this means I'm not going to Harvard?" I asked.

Mr. Schwartz removed his glasses, then leafed briefly through my records, in a manila folder on his desk. "You have perfect SATs," he said. You have a 5.0 grade point average. You placed extremely high in the International Math Olympiad. You are on the School math team. Very, very impressive. Extremely impressive. Ordinarily you would be shoo-in for Harvard."

"But this is not <u>ordinarily</u>," I completed his thought.

"This is not ordinarily," he said.

"So what are my chances?" I asked.

"In the best of times Harvard accepts about five percent of 30,000 or more students who apply. But, now, because of the mandatory preferences of the Victims Law, many more will apply. So if 100,000 apply, and Harvard takes only 1500, and eighty percent must be Victims, do the math."

I did the math. "So what do I do?" I asked. "Going to Harvard has been my dream for years."

Mr. Schwartz shook his head. "I don't know, son. I don't know. Send in your application and pray."

At that moment I knew what my senior hack would be – and also that I would stand for election to the Lords of Hack.

3

When I told my parents about my meeting with Mr. Schwartz, they were predictably upset. Going to Harvard was not just my dream; it was also theirs.

"I knew it!" yelled my father. "I knew no good would come of that law! This is what you get when Democrats swept 2016! One-party control is never good for this country!"

My mother was sullenly silent. She was a die-hard Democrat. Her dream of social justice had just taken a wrong turn.

I recalled now the dinner-table debates I had tuned out when the Victims Law was passing Congress.

My mother had argued, of course, that the V-Law was the final jewel in the crown of social justice for minorities – recompense for all groups who had been trampled by the American Dream! My father, to his credit, said it would create an American Apartheid.

"Aparthheid?" my mother had said. "What a terrible thing! How is that possible in America? You're a Jew! Jews have always stood for Civil Rights and social justice. We are the good guys! You always tell me you're an Independent! What are you turning into - a

Republican? Apartheid! Apartheid! You sound like a racist!" She was very upset.

That had been their last discussion of the Victims Law. Now – now - we were feeling, firsthand, the effect.

Meanwhile, given my earlier third and second prizes I was easily elected a Lord of Hack. (Many hackers voted for me to make sure I would not compete against them!)

The election took me out of the competition – and thus out of the limelight. Now I would not have to answer questions about what hack I was doing.

I threw myself into classes, some interesting, some not. I thought about entering the Xxiel Science Competition but decided it would be a waste of time. If I were right, it would not matter.

When the time came, I completed and filed the application to Harvard. It was not hard; since the whole thing was on-line, there were not a lot of documents.

Although it was a uniform application, one submission for all U.S. colleges, I checked the box for only one school – Harvard. When people asked about my "safety" schools, I lied. I said I had applied to Yale, Princeton, and Dartmouth.

There was, of course, the college essay. Most students wrote about helping in a homeless shelter, or organizing a fundraiser to stop global warming, or being a summer intern at a Nairobi birthing hospice.

Since it made no difference, I wrote about Srinivasa Ramanujan, the autodidact math genius, born in Madras, who (among other honors) became a Fellow of Trinity College, Cambridge. In the essay I sketched his life and explained how his story and discoveries had resonated with me since my earliest interest in math.

Thereafter the fall semester droned on, and I focused on my personal, outside-the-competition hack. The idea was simple - crack Harvard's admission files and change my "non-acceptance" to "acceptance".

It seemed so obvious to me, and I was anxious to do it. Yet I needed patience; and patience was not my strength.

Why patience? Because, for the real all-or-nothing hack, I must wait until Harvard had made - but not yet published - its final admission decisions, which were still several months away.

In the interim I had planning to do. Experience had taught me a difficult hack could take three or four weeks - and I assumed Harvard would be very difficult. I would need to do some practice runs. So, as soon as I filed my college application, I began testing Harvard's cyber-moats.

There was of course the remote, <u>very remote</u>, chance that Harvard might accept me. In that event, if I had already hacked into their system, I would simply walk away. But, under the Victims Law, that acceptance was a long shot. I guessed my odds were just slightly better than winning the lottery.

When I started to probe, I found that the Harvard cyber-walls were high and wide, so to speak - but nothing I had not seen before. In fact, Harvard used the same big-bank standard security protocols that I had already cracked in my junior year. Could it be that easy?

There were, of course, two new risks because of the Victims Law. What were these risks?

First, since they now controlled <u>all</u> college admissions, the feds might watch the Harvard admission process. Thus federal eyes might be scanning Harvard's system and watching for intruders. (Why didn't I think this outrageous? Because everyone knew the NSA watched all emails and phone calls anyway.)

Second, it was likely a federal crime, somewhere in the 1,000-plus-page Victims Law, to do what I was doing. But so was hacking a bank. Yet I was not worried. I had the supreme confidence of youth; I knew I would not be caught.

The main reason I had to delay the actual Harvard hack was that I was not applying for early admission. Early admission was the process where you told Harvard (or your other first choice) that, if accepted, you would say "yes".

Even before the V-Law, early admission was attacked as elitist and racist, because it iced almost half the acceptances, making it harder for those who did not apply early - and, it was argued, minority students. Hence the V-Law now required a phase-out of early admissions over the next two years.

While this was only the first year of the early-admission phase-out, I guessed early applications would get still get extra federal scrutiny. It would be better, I thought, to swim in the 'ordinary' pool.

I decided, however, that early admission would be a good test run for the Harvard hack. Perhaps I could also 'help out' a friend who was applying early to Harvard.

So, in December, one week before the early admission announcements, I cracked Harvard's files. As expected from my practice runs, it was a surprisingly simple hack, no big deal. I got in easily and was soon scanning the Harvard decisions.

Harvard organized its files by race, gender, sexual preference, religion - and school. This made it easy. Finding the Stuyvesant file, I saw 20 early applications from our senior class. There were three acceptances and 17 rejections. The acceptances were an African-American boy, a Chinese girl, and a Muslim boy. The two boys had SAT scores near the bottom of our class. The Chinese girl had very high scores.

The files showed no reason for acceptance or rejection. This was surprising but positive; it meant that changing a file would not require re-writing the justification for rejection. It would be easy, therefore, to change the decision for any applicant.

The friend whom I wanted to help had been rejected. But, as I started to change his result, I caught myself. It was too risky. Suppose Harvard or the feds found the hack; they would immediately heighten security - and perhaps block me from changing my own file later.

Even worse, they might investigate my friend, who was innocent. I did not want to wreck his future. Sobered, I left the Harvard system without a leaving a footfall.

4

With the final college decisions set for April 14th, time seemed to slow down. The weeks were interminable. I focused on course work but found it hard to concentrate. Only being a Lord of Hack created some daylight.

In the prior years when I was competing in the annual Hack, a few classmates told me about their hacks; yet I could never have guessed at the sheer cleverness or number of the Stuy student hacks. As a Lord of Hack, I now had a front row seat to a showing of unbelievable creativity.

There were two parts to the Hack competition. To save the Lords from reviewing complete details of a thousand hacks, students were required, in the first stage, to submit an outline - no more than 250 words - of their hack. From these outlines the Lords picked 100 finalists.

Then, in the second stage, the 100 finalists would complete their hacks, which the Lords would then judge on technical complexity and success of execution.

The first-round outlines were due the same week I cracked the Harvard early-admission files.

Each of us Lords took one-third of the first-round outlines to grade and then discuss with the other Lords. We would then meet to discuss the result our grading.

To ensure due process, each decision, pro or con, required a vote at least two Lords. (Since students are always super-concerned about fairness, we wanted the process to be as fair as possible.)

We had received 1230 submissions; so we each had to review 400 or so. I decided to read my batch in a single weekend.

Needing a quiet place, and not wanting nosy questions from my parents, I went to the Reading Room of The New York Public Library, one of my favorite places in New York. Camped there for a Saturday, I opened my comp-pad and dove into what I expected would be a tedious task.

It was indeed, as I expected, a tedious task; but I quickly organized it in an efficient way to move things along.

After reading a few outlines, I saw three clear categories. There were obvious finalists, and obvious rejects, and what I called the "gray middle." In the "grey middle" were those I did not love but could not immediately reject.

With this sorting method, I made a first pass. The result: 60 finalists, 276 rejects, and 41 gray middlers.

I then made a second pass through the gray middle. Most, this time, were rejects. If a hack was not an obvious finalist, I decided, it must be a reject. I did, however, find six obvious finalists whom I missed the first time around.

Who was an obvious finalist or an obvious reject?

One clear finalist wanted to hack NSA's metadata files and find his own NSA file. That was awesome! One clear reject wanted to hack FaceBook and find sexy pictures of girls that had been deleted from the public file. Not awesome.

The whole task took all of a Saturday - and then part of a Sunday working at home.

In the end I made a spreadsheet of my choices to email the other Lords. Then, as I was wrapping up, I noticed something.

One of my finalists was the Chinese girl whose name I had seen in the Harvard early acceptance files! Her name was Sarah Po.

Not many girls did the Hack - indeed, there were not many girl hackers anywhere. The reasons for this can be left to the sociologists. It was, however, an accepted fact - so accepted that I went back to look at the outline Po had submitted. I wanted to see a clever girl's hack.

Po was very clever indeed. She planned to hack Chinese government files to learn what happened to her great grandfather, a high Party functionary who had disappeared without a trace. Such a hack would require great talent to execute, to say nothing of knowing Mandarin.

Po's hack resonated with me, although I did not know why.

The next week we Lords met to decide the finalists. At my urging Po got three votes, not just the requisite two.

We notified the competitors by email of their results. We sent the emails from a secure overseas web address that the Lords created anew each year for the competition. I wondered how Po reacted to the news.

Although Po was a senior, I did not know her - not strange in such a large class. Girls were slightly less than forty percent of our class. This was because, even under the City's Working People's Party, acceptance to Stuy was still based on standardized tests (required by State law, which the WFP had been unable to get changed). Despite years of pushing to get girls into mathematics, math was still mainly a male thing.

With the first-round Hack selections done, time now sped up. I tried to bury myself in classwork. Not a day passed, however, when I did not think about my upcoming Harvard hack.

5

Soon it was the first week in April, one week before Harvard would announce its decisions. It was time for my bet-the-future hack.

To be safe (as we had done for the Hack emails), I had created a blind offshore computer account. I hoped the feds could not trace me from a Bogota email address!) From this distant portal, I cracked into the Harvard files.

As before, I easily penetrated the standard cyber-walls but then had a shock! I was blocked by a new and very weird gate!

It was a lattice-like code structure of a type I had never seen before. "Oh, fuck! Fuck! Fuck!" I yelled. (I was sitting in the New York Public Library Reading Room; my outburst drew stares.)

What now? There was one week before Harvard sent out its decisions; to allow myself a margin for error I had at best three days to crack the lattice code.

Staring at my comp-pad, I took a deep breath. Then I dove back into the Harvard files looking for openings or flaws.

I found none - no openings or flaws.

Then I tried some time-tested 'end-around' strategies. Nothing worked.

I started to panic but caught myself. Panic was the enemy; being calm would be necessary to beat such a challenge.

To crack the Harvard lattice code I had to stay calm and focused. I had to believe - as my parents always drilled into me - that there was nothing to fear but fear itself. I hoped FDR had been right.

Guessing I would not crack the lattice code that day, I left the Library and walked up Fifth Avenue. It was a warm spring day when New York was at its best.

As I walked, I let my thoughts run. Sometimes not thinking about a problem would lead to a solution; my subconscious often gave me the right answer after a good night's sleep. Right now, however, walking in Fifth Avenue sunlight did not jog my subconscious. Maybe the answer would come later.

That night, before going to sleep, I made notes about the mathematical structure of a lattice. It was just a series of repetitions, expanding geometrically in all directions. I thought of a lattice fence around a garden. Maybe a lattice fence would give the answer.

When I finally fell asleep, I had a series of crazy dreams about huge walls blocking me whichever way I turned. I awoke upset and confused.

It was 3 a.m. I was really tired and wondered if I could get back to sleep. Then, unexpectedly, I dropped into a deep and restful sleep.

Deep in that new sleep I dreamt about endless lattices stretching to the ends of the universe. In the dream a silver skeleton key moved back and forth among the thousands of lattices.

I was so deep in the dream that I slept through my morning alarm. Awakening, I remembered the dream with incredible clarity; but the answer still eluded me. I had two days left to crack the Harvard code.

Classes that day were a blur. I was supposed to meet the other Lords in the afternoon at Starbucks; instead, I begged off and rushed uptown to the Library. Finding my usual corner of the Reading Room, I dove back into the Harvard files.

The lattice code was still there, blocking my future, saying, "You will not go to Harvard!" I stared and stared. Then I remembered the skeleton key from my dream. What was a key for? A key opened a lock, of course!

And that was the answer, staring me in the face. There must be a lock! The lattice must have a lock that opened with a key.

I studied the lattices more closely. They did seem to stretch endlessly in all directions; but there must be a single entry point, a door. No one (at least in the Spring of 2018) could yet create a complex structure without a door.

I looked at my notes from the previous night. They included the math formula for a repeating lattice, which in fact was not that complicated - merely repetitious. I stared at the formula; then, in a second, remembering the skeleton key from my dream, I derived the location of the entry point.

I looked at the code on the screen. Working the new formula, I quickly confirmed the entry point. The skeleton key had been right.

At the entry point I was asked for a password.

But what was the password?

I thought of the Harvard seal and motto, "Veritas." The password could not be that simple. But guess what? It was. After creating an incredibly complex code, the author had played a joke. The password was indeed "Veritas". (Hubris leads to error. He must have assumed no one would <u>ever</u> find the door. He had not expected me.) I "turned the key" and was in.

The rest was easy. I changed my "non-acceptance" to "acceptance". (I had of course been rejected). The following week I received my admission letter.

I was going to Harvard.

6

It remained only to judge the finals of the Hack competition. With the Harvard ordeal behind me, the Hack finals were fun.

We required each finalist to give a fifteen-minute oral presentation to the Lords of Hack. (There were now sixteen finalists after we had graded the results of the actual, completed hacks of the first-round finalists.) Each finalist had submitted a one-page summary of their completed hack, plus a sample of their programming or code creation. From these submissions we picked the final round of sixteen "final" finalists.

Needless to say, we went off-campus for these final presentations, which we held on a Saturday morning. Our site was a small conference room in the law firm where the father of one of the other Lords was a partner. It would be a long, but interesting, day.

All sixteen had done great work. For example, one had hacked the farm subsidy files of the U.S. Department of Agriculture. Another had cracked an online-Broadway ticket seller and sent five tickets for the revival of "Annie" to a Bronx orphanage. And so on.

Po was the twelfth to present. After eleven interviews, despite the cleverness of each one of the final hacks, I was starting to fade. I had actually forgotten she was a finalist until she walked in. Then, feeling a charge of electricity, I sat up straight.

She was striking - about five four, with that wonderful long Chinese black hair, bright brown eyes, horn-rimmed glasses, and a curvy figure hidden under a white blouse and black trousers. Her clothes were cool but gave an impression of Chinese classical dress.

She had a very unusual necklace with six different-shaped green pieces. Unable to stop staring at her, I had trouble concentrating on her presentation.

Po described her hack calmly in a low soprano voice, with short pauses for emphasis.

True to her initial proposal, she had indeed hacked the files of the Chinese Communist Party; and she had indeed found the file on her lost great grandfather.

She said he had been taken into "protective custody" in 1952 and then sent to a "Re-Education Camp" in Eastern Mongolia. He died six months later, probably from malnutrition and pneumonia.

"And what was his crime?" Po ended. "He made a joke about Chairman Mao at a private party!" But there was, of course, no such thing as a private party in China. At any social gathering there was <u>always</u> an informer present; and even a simple joke by a very high party functionary - her grandfather - was reported and punished.

"Sounds like the InAp List," I blurted out. The others looked at me with surprise. We all knew the InAp List was bullshit; but even our small group, sneakily engaged in illicit activity, was uncomfortable joking about the InAp List.

The three of us had sat riveted through Po's presentation. At the end we thanked her and gave her our standard answer – she had been great; we had a tough job to decide on the three finalists; we would announce the results in about a week.

After Po left, it was a struggle to stay awake for the last four finalists. At the end we picked the top five (of which Po was one) and agreed to meet again during the next week to make the final selections.

7

I forgot to mention that college admissions that year were the worst in Stuyvesant history, although almost every African-American, Hispanic, female, and gay student got their first choice. (More of our classmates were gay, we learned, than anyone would have believed. There were a lot of jokes about "admission gays".)

Most non-Victims, including many of the brightest students, not only failed to get their first choice; they did not get into <u>any</u> college. The school was in shock.

Since Stuy was a City public school, and with the added threat of the InAp List, the faculty was afraid to criticize, or even speak about, the Victims Law. Yet the effect was clear. Why would the City's smartest kids compete for Stuyvesant, with its legendary rigor, with no possible chance of good college admissions? One shocking – if predictable - effect of the Victims Law was now clear.

Given its disastrous results, Stuyvesant decided that year not to publish its college acceptances. This helped me because I wanted to keep my Harvard admission as quiet as possible.

I had told no one about getting into Harvard. Given my classmates' grim results, I did not want to draw attention to my astounding good luck. Although my parents knew, of course, I did not even confide in my friends. If asked, I said that I had been wait-listed for Harvard and Yale.

Even being wait-listed was a plus, compared to the rejections many had received. Also, I downplayed my chances of moving up the wait-list, saying it was just luck-of-the-draw and that I had no real hope.

By the end of summer I would confide in a few close friends. At that point Stuyvesant would already be focused on the new school year, and I would (I hoped) be forgotten.

Of course, Mr. Schwartz, my college counselor, got the news. When he called me to his office to offer congratulations, he said, in a moment of candor, that I must be one of the token non-Victims – and, if so, that Harvard could not have picked a better token. I asked him, as a favor, not to discuss my unbelievable luck with anyone else. Pondering my request, he looked at me thoughtfully. He said he understood and would keep it under his hat.

The rest of the school year went quickly. We gave Po second place in the competition. While her hack was amazing, the winner had hacked into NASA's files and actually changed the coordinates of a far galaxy. Since it would be a while before anyone lost their way in that galaxy, we gave him first place.

At graduation I won the math prize. I was not valedictorian, however, (to my parents' great chagrin) because I got a 4.7 in German, ruining my perfect average.

Some classmates jokingly asked how I blew it. I said that becoming fluent in the language of the Oppressor took work. One of them cracked, "Arbeit Macht Frei", which was not funny.

8

And so to Harvard.

Cambridge in early fall is wonderful, red and yellow leaves falling in the Yard and in the House courtyards, clear and crisp nights, students returning in good spirit with the high promise of a new academic year.

I had a double room in Wigglesworth, the old three-story brick dormitory that runs along Massachusetts Avenue behind Widener Library. My roommate was a Jewish boy from Brooklyn - Ari Cohen, a graduate of Bronx Science, another elite New York City high school.

The first thing we discussed was our amazing luck at avoiding the dead hand of the Victims Law. Ari told me immediately that he was pre-med. He said that if he did anything else his mother would kill him.

"What's the shortest telephone call?" Ari asked me. Before I could answer, he said, "Max, a Jewish boy, dials his mother's number. The phone rings and a woman answers, "Hello?" "Ma", says Max, "How are you?" "Oh, I'm fine, just fine," says the woman. "Sorry!" says Max, "wrong number!" And he hangs up."

Thus began a Harvard year in which the six-foot, skinny, bespectacled Ari would keep me laughing day and night. Drawing from a well of Yiddish humor absorbed in yeshiva years before Bronx Science, he had scores of centuries-old jokes.

On that first day, after disclosing his pre-med major, he asked what I would major in. "Math," I said. "Math is my thing. Has been ever since I was a kid."

"O.K.," he said. "Math is good. If you aren't going to be a doctor or a lawyer, why not a mathematician? Except, how do mathematicians make a living?"

I had never really considered the point. I assumed the future would take care of itself. I said people needed mathematicians for serious computer stuff, among other things.

"Are you observant?" Ari asked, switching the topic.

"Not," I answered. I said that my parents were secular Jews, not even Reform, although they had insisted that I be bar mitzvah. Since then, however, I had never been to a synagogue.

"Like the Rabbi's mice," said Ari, and he told this joke.

"An old rabbi had a small, poor shul in Eastern Europe. The shul suddenly had a mice infestation. The threadbare congregants were beside themselves. The mice climbed all over; their scampering even interrupted Shabbos prayers. The desperate rabbi prayed for a solution, and the Lord gave him the answer."

"Next Shabbos morning the rabbi put a huge chunk of cheese on the bimah. The mice immediately climbed up and attacked the cheese. Then, while the mice were busily stuffing themselves, the rabbi made them all bar mitzvah. After their bar mitzvah, of course, the mice immediately left the shul and never came back."

"So, are you observant?" I asked, "after eight years of yeshiva?"

"Not so much," said Ari. "Bronx Science corrupted me; but I still believe, and I go to shul on Friday nights."

"Then you can't go to any mixers," I said.

"They have them on Saturday nights, too," Ari said. "Besides, you meet some hot girls at Friday night services. There is nothing hotter than a Jewish girl who thinks she is being religious. Believe me, I will be your Moses and lead you to the Promised Land!"

I wasn't sure about that. I suggested we try a mixer the coming Saturday night, if for no other reason than to start getting to know Harvard.

"Only if you come to Friday night services first," said Ari. "I'm telling you - wait and see!"

I agreed, reluctantly.

Before Friday, however, we had to check out, and sign up for, our fall courses. This did not turn out as I had expected.

All Harvard students were required to take Core Curriculum - meaning courses in the major subject categories that would lead to a well-rounded education. Because I had very, very advanced placement in math, I assumed I could skip boring Core courses. I was wrong. The course-selection website insisted I take introductory courses in history, English, science, and the social sciences.

When I griped to my Freshman Adviser at our first meeting, she chided me. Because of the Victims Law, Harvard had changed the curriculum. They increased the Core requirements and, as affecting me, reduced by half the number of high-level math courses. The faculty's new Victims Law Committee had decided that high-level math was too elitist.

"Also too much money for a handful of non-Victim students," she told me. Her name was Gerta Weg-Rafl. Herself a mathematician, she had been a non-tenured Assistant Professor for many years. She did not love Harvard's administration. "You will have to do complex math in your spare time," she said.

I left that meeting really pissed. Maybe I should have gone to MIT. Then I realized MIT would probably have similar problems. How would the Victims Law impact a school where science and math <u>were</u> the core curriculum?

Surrendering to the Harvard website, I picked the few Core courses I thought might be remotely interesting. And I did get one mid-level math course.

By then it was Friday, and I was at loose ends. For four years I had focused total energy on getting into Harvard. Now I was here. What to do next?

I met Ari for dinner at Annenberg, the huge freshman dining hall. He was in a great mood. He had managed to get into Biochemistry, one of the few freshmen to do so.

I told him about my failed attempt to get a high-level math course. We both assumed that even under the Victims Law the country still needed doctors, and doctors needed biochemistry. Unfortunately, the medical profession did not need higher math.

Ari asked what I was doing after dinner. "Nothing," I said.

"Good," he said. "It's time for Friday night services – remember?"

The last thing I wanted was to attend services. But I had nothing to do; and I remembered what Ari had said about hot Jewish girls. "O.K.," I said. "What the hell."

"Shabbat shalom!" said Ari, and off we went to services.

Harvard's Friday night services for reform and conservative students were held in Memorial Church, the grand example of New England plain church architecture that sits in Harvard Yard.

It was a fine, clear fall night. There were small groups of students sitting on the Widener Library steps or lingering in the Yard.

As we approached Mem Church, we saw a group of people picketing outside. The picketers were a motley bunch, some with Muslim skullcaps, others looking like hippies, Gothies, etc. Holding their signs high, they marched slowly in a staggered circle; weirdly, they were totally silent.

As we got closer, we saw that their signs had anti-Israel rants. "Nazi Zionists out of Palestine!" said one. "Punish the Israeli War Criminals!" said another. "BDS! Boycott, Divestment, Sanctions! Divest from Israel now!" said a third.

The leader was a tall boy with a full-face Muslim beard. It just happened that his circling path came close to us as we passed. Pausing to stop and stare at Ari and me, he glowered at us with sheer hatred. It was not the warmest reception for Friday night services.

Ari and I responded with angry stares of our own. Then, looking at each other but saying nothing, we continued past the picketers and into Mem Church.

This was not the Harvard I expected.

Both furious, we walked down the aisle and stepped into a row of pews not far from the front. I went in first.

I was outraged. Growing up in New York City, a Jewish town, and attending Stuyvesant, I had never experienced anti-Semitism, let alone outright hatred. I was so angry I did not notice the three girls sitting next to me.

51

"If it isn't a Lord of Hack!" said a female voice next to me. "Good Shabbos!"

Still dazed by the picketers, I did not respond.

"I said, hello, Lord of Hack!" the girl repeated.

I turned to the voice. It was Sarah Po! Now I was rattled for another reason. I lost my power of speech.

"I bet you wonder what a Chinese girl is doing at Friday night services?" she said. Her voice had a bell in it, one of the most wonderful chimes I had ever heard.

Recovering, and trying to be chill, I smiled and said, "Yes, indeed! Of course! Absolutely! And why would I not wonder that?"

"Because, you see," she said, "I'm Jewish! My mother is Jewish and my father Chinese -which makes me all Jewish and half Chinese!"

"Now that is really cool," was all I could say. "But which half is which?" I asked.

"I know, but I never tell," she answered, with a bright smile that took away my breath.

At that moment the service began. Summoning a courage I did not know I had, I whispered, "Want to get a coffee at Starbuck's after the service?"

"Love to," she said, which left me, for the rest of the service, in a complete daze.

9

I will never forget that night. It was one of those amazing Cambridge fall nights; the sky was crystal blue-black, and all futures were possible.

After so many years I still remember the clarity of that night.

We wound up, five of us, Sarah and her two friends, and Ari and me, at Starbucks after the service.

I don't remember the conversation. I do remember we sat at two adjoining tables with five chairs pulled around and talked the usual Harvard freshman talk.

The two girls were Sarah's roommates in Holworthy. After prolonging the coffee as long as we could, Ari and I walked them back to their dorm. I walked with Sarah, Ari with the other girls.

Sarah said she had the same problem I did in trying for advanced math. She had also wound up with really dull Core courses.

When I told her what my Adviser said about doing complex math on my own, she perked up. "Why don't we do problems together?" she asked. "We could meet once a week and do sets we thought we would get in the advanced courses?"

The Lord was truly watching over me that night. As Ari's mother might have said, it was meant to be.

I answered immediately that it was a great idea - of course we should do math together. We agreed to meet the coming Monday afternoon on the bank of the Charles across from Winthrop House.

For the rest of the weekend I could think only of Sarah's face.

Who could have known that math problems could be incredibly sexy? From that first meeting in Mem Church, of course, there was an electric charge between Sarah and me, and we both knew it.

Sitting on the riverbank, with the current flowing under the nearby Weeks Bridge, we did actually do math problems. But there was no denying this other thing, this electricity.

Sarah had a really fine math mind. She said her father had started her with numbers when she was three, and by the time she was nine she was doing calculus.

Getting into Stuyvesant had been easy. Her math ability also opened the door to Harvard (and Yale and

Princeton, which also accepted her). The Victims Law gave her a big advantage, despite her Chinese name.

A girl with advanced math was a shoo-in wherever she applied. Chinese were not Victims, she added, although it was well known that there were unwritten quotas on Chinese college admissions under the Victims Law even though the regulations did not say so. But a girl with advanced math would beat any quotas.

For the next three weeks we met at least one afternoon by the river. Time stood still. We sat on a blanket and discussed the most complex problems we could find in the math universe, all the while knowing it was not about the math.

One Friday night I took Sarah to a movie, and one night we took the "T" into Boston and had dinner at O'Pietro, a small Italian restaurant in the North End. Since we both had roommates and Spartan budgets, we had no chance to be together in private.

Then the chance came. Ari decided to go home for the Jewish holidays. It was not actually a decision, he joked, but a maternal commandment. "What - you would even think of not coming home for the holidays?" his mother asked. Thus, thanks to Mrs. Cohen, I would have the room in Wigglesworth to myself for an entire weekend.

I told Sarah that Ari would be away and asked if she wanted to come over Saturday afternoon. She did not hesitate for a nanosecond to say yes.

What happened that Saturday afternoon and the rest of the weekend was magical.

My only experiences with women had been occasional visits to a few establishments in New York's financial district that catered to Stuyvesant boys. I had never had an adult relationship with a woman my age.

Sarah was also inexperienced. She was a virgin, and not just because her parents had been strict. Being as smart as she was, and skeptical of militant feminism, she had believed in waiting for the real thing, not just getting "experience".

Which meant I was the real thing.

Whatever our inexperience, we so immersed ourselves in each other that weekend that I wondered how I could ever go back to normal life.

Sunday morning we took a long walk around Cambridge, hand-in-hand, saying nothing. I guess we went out to eat, but I don't remember much.

What I remember, even so many years later, is Sarah's glossy black hair and beautiful body.

It was an idyll everyone should have at least once in life. It was why writers write, and painters paint, and singers sing. It was amazing.

I also learned the story of Sarah's unusual six-piece green necklace, which she rarely removed.

It was jade, an heirloom her father's family had managed to keep and hand down, generation to generation - wars, Chairman Mao, and the Cultural Revolution notwithstanding. No one knew its true age.

"The six pieces represent the sky, the earth, and the four directions," said Sarah. "And jade also represents purity and harmony. My family calls this necklace the 'Six Green Harmony.' Now it is mine to keep safe and pass on."

I guessed that the necklace represented more than Sarah was saying, but I did not ask further.

Our dream together continued in slow motion through a sunny Sunday afternoon and into an autumn evening that seemed as if it would never end. When Sarah left that night to return to Holworthy, I knew my life had changed forever.

It was a shock - a jolting shock - therefore, returning to Monday morning reality, to read the <u>Crimson</u> headline about the new DNA "pin-prick" test.

(The Crimson was Harvard's daily newspaper, delivered to the door every morning.)

Apparently the federal government was having huge trouble dealing with paperwork for the Victims Law.[*] The Department of Health and Human Services, which was supposed to administer the law, was overwhelmed (like what happened with ObamaCare, said the Crimson writer).

Huge numbers of people were claiming to be African-American, Hispanic, Native American, or gay. Under the V-Law law everyone received a certificate showing his or her Victim (or non-Victim) category. For race and ethnicity, this category depended on the status of your four grandparents.

So, if you had three African-American grandparents and one white, you were three-fourths African-American - meaning that you got a three-fourths preference, as opposed to a full preference for a person with four African-American grandparents.

You might also have a half-preference or a quarter-preference. Also, there were different credit categories for different ethnicities. For example,

---

[*] I forgot to mention that everyone had earlier been required to file a form with DHHS identifying your parents and grandparents and checking boxes for each person's ethnicity, race, and gender.

African-Americans got full credits; Hispanics and Native Americans, two-thirds credits; and gays and women, half-credits.

Multiply these calculations by millions, and for different categories, add that it was a government-managed program, and you will understand the confusion. Throw in that it was difficult to disprove that someone was gay, and it was even worse. The ObamaCare start-up was kindergarten in comparison.

You will understand, also, the impossibility of using a self-certification system. There was massive fraud.

To deal with all these complexities, and to defeat that fraud, the government had announced that it would now require a pinprick test of DNA to determine your rightful Victim category.

Also, according to the Crimson, management of the V- Law had now been transferred to the National Security Agency - the "NSA", which the President said was better equipped to deal "responsibly" with the "important data needs" of the Victims Law.

There would be no more self-certifications, on-line or on paper.

Now every American must report annually for the DNA test. They would prick your finger and take a drop of blood. Your DNA would be logged into the NSA database. You would receive your Victim Certificate - your "V-Cert" - via email, and that would be that. And, of course, your DNA, with all its identifying characteristics and genetic map, would now be forever in that federal database.

That Monday's Crimson had two editorials, one pro and one con.

The "pro" editorial argued that the V-Law was the culmination of decades of struggle for social justice in America. The pinprick test, it said, was the perfect use of technology to stop the increasing outrageous abuses of V-Law preferences by fraudsters gaming the system.

The "con" editorial said the pinprick test was another nail in the coffin of American liberty. "Any illusion of privacy is now a fantasy," wrote the author. "Will they now divide us by one-eighth ancestral blood? By one-sixteenth? How many new categories of Victims will we have? We lost America when the President signed the V- Law. Now we are hopelessly lost."

After classes that Monday morning I met Sarah at Annenberg. I brought The Crimson, which she had not yet seen. She blanched when she read the pinprick story and the editorials.

"This is what happened in China," she said. "Only this is worse - much, much worse. Can you imagine Chairman Mao with the ability to get everyone's DNA?"

10

Two weeks later we received notice to report to the Harvard Health Services for our pinpricks. On the appointed day Sarah, Ari, and I went together.

Outside HHS the line of students stretched down along Mt. Auburn Street. Unlike most such student lines, this one was dead silent. Nobody joked or spoke. (I remembered the silence in the Stuyvesant auditorium as we filed out after learning that the V-Law had changed college acceptance rules.)

We knew our world had changed. We were not sure what would come next, but it could not be good.

The actual DNA pinprick was nothing. We showed our Harvard I.D. to the nurse; she logged us into her computer, pricked a fingertip, and took a drop of blood with a needle linked by line to a machine. The machine beeped, indicating that the sample was transmitted, and we were done.

Walking out into sunshine, I said to Sarah that something of great value had been taken from us.

"Don't let it get you down," she said. "Think of it as nothing. A leaf of nothing falling into the celestial pool."

"That sounds like your Chinese grandmother," I said.

"Of course," she said. "How did you know?"

We held hands as we walked back to the Yard. But I knew, I had a feeling in my bones, that it was not a leaf of nothing.

The next week we received emails from the NSA. Sarah's included a Victim Certificate (a "V-Cert"), because she was a woman. The V-Cert identified her as female heterosexual. It said her ancestry was 25% Beijing Chinese, 25% Shanghai Chinese, and 50% Ashkenzi Jew.

My email included a Non-Victim Certificate (or "Non-V Cert"). It identified me as male heterosexual and 100% Ashkenazi Jew.

"At least now I know for sure," joked Ari, who got the same Non-V Cert as I did. "I always thought I was a Yid; but it must be true if the NSA says I am!"

We both wondered why we were identified as Jewish, not just Caucasian.

There was nothing in the V-Law about Jews.

Everyone wondered how a DNA test could show sexual orientation. The Crimson gave the answer.

Testing was now so sophisticated, it reported, that it could show gender orientation with more than 85% accuracy.

Because the test was not 100% accurate, however, if a gay man or woman received a V-Cert showing him or her as straight, they could file a supplemental application for their V-Cert. This application, quickly known as the "Gay Supp," required documentary proof. This meant the same crude test that had been used to disqualify gays from the Vietnam War. The applicant must include a photo showing him or her engaged in gay sex, a requirement that - said The Crimson - was expected to cut down fake applications.

Courses ended, and Reading Period began (the three-week period before exams when Harvard allows students to do the reading you should have done during the semester). However dreary the Core courses, I could not break my study habit of so many years. I plowed through the reading hoping to get my usual "A"s.

Later, at the first exam, I was surprised that I had to sign my exam book not only with my student number but also my Victim status – or, in my case, Non-V status. Why did they need V status to grade an exam? Not a good thing, for sure.

Two weeks later a Crimson story answered that question. New V-Law regulations required all universities to give separate grades to Victims by category. This was to ensure fairness in grading for Victims and to stop professors from grading Victims according to improper, elite standards.

"Don't worry," said Sarah. "You'll still get your "A"s. After all, you and Ari both got into Harvard despite the V- Law. Nothing will change for you."

Although Sarah and I were closer than heartbeats, I had not told her about my Harvard hack. Her comment piqued my interest about Ari, however. Ari and I had both joked about the V-Law. I still wondered how he had gotten in to Harvard.

That night, as we finished studying, I asked him. "Ari," I said, "how did you get in to Harvard? How did you win the lottery?"

Ari looked at me quizzically. "Probably the same way you did," he said. "I applied. And I also asked eighteen rabbis to pray for me. Obviously it was the magic '18'". He paused. "What about you?"

"The same," I said. "Only in my case it was three Democrats. Three Democrats are equal to eighteen rabbis."

"I thought Democrats don't believe in God," Ari said.

We both laughed, and the discussion ended, at least for then.

I did get all "A"s that semester - in the new non-V category, which left me with a strange taste in my mouth. Sarah also got straight "A"s - in the new Women Victim category.

"See," Sarah said, "I told you not to worry." But my foreboding remained.

11

It was now February in Cambridge, the deepest dark of winter. Just as Cambridge delights in autumn and spring, it depresses in dingy mid-winter. Snow alternates with rain and sleet; everything is gritty gray and mostly freezing. Only the occasional big snow, creating a high snow bank day, affords emotional relief.

Sarah and I now faced the problem of what to do during the summer. I did not want her away by herself on some or other internship, and she felt the same about me.

Neither of us had told our parents about our relationship; but neither of us could afford an apartment on our own. With the terrible economy, summer jobs were not just scarce but virtually non-existent.

I should have known, however, that a brilliant woman would get first choice of the few available jobs. Unbelievably but predictably, Sarah got not one, but two, offers of good summer work.

The one she accepted was working for a Boston actuarial company. The job actually paid a salary, enough for her to share a cheap apartment if we could find one - and if I could pay the other half share.

I had no such luck.

As a Non-Victim, I was at the end of every possible hiring list. All employers, big and small, outdid themselves in hiring Victims, because they had to file quarterly reports with the NSA. That left not even crumbs for Non-Vs. After twelve immediate rejections to my on-line applications, I was depressed.

Then a miracle happened. I saw a short note on a bulletin board in the Math Department. (I went to the Math offices at least once a week just for the hell of it.)

The note read simply, "Professor needs research assistant to help with computer language project for summer. See Professor P. Stavisky." The address given was in one of Harvard's older science buildings.

With an hour between classes, I ran to the address in the Professor's note and looked for his office, "Room 021". After walking around the first floor, I figured out that "0" meant the basement and, finding a staircase, walked down one flight.

Room 021 was at the end of a long hallway and around a corner. On the door was a small nameplate: "Professor Pyotr Stavisky". I knocked.

"Enter," said a voice.

Inside was a vast clutter of papers and books strewn around the floor and in plywood bookshelves. Behind a battered desk sat the professor.

Pyotr Stavisky looked to be in his late fifties or early sixties, a giant of a man, with long hair, academic spectacles, and rumpled gray worker's shirt. He had a long-stemmed pipe in his mouth, turned upside down, which he chewed absent-mindedly like old gum. In front of him on the desk were a desktop computer, a laptop, and a comp-pad.

"Yes," he said. "What do you want? I hope it's not another question about this week's assignment!" He was not inclined to conversation. He had a slight Russian accent.

"It's about your notice," I said. "The summer research project. On the bulletin boards."

"Oh, that," he said. "Do you know how many applicants I have had for that job? And not one could unscramble a one from a zero!" He grimaced.

"Try me," I said.

With a skeptical look he reached back and took a piece of paper from a shelf behind him. "Write down your answers to the list of questions on this paper. Then come back and read them to me. If you take more than half an hour, you automatically fail."

I scanned the questions. "If you let me sit down, I will give you the answers now," I said.

This challenge got his interest. He motioned me to sit on one of two chairs in front of his desk, which I did after moving a stack of papers to the floor.

"So," he said, "what are the answers?"

It took all of eight minutes. I gave him a complete and correct answer to every one of his questions.

He listened with increasing focus as I spoke. When I finished, he said simply, "You're hired! By the way, who are you?"

I introduced myself, said I was a freshman majoring in math, and really needed a job for the summer. I said I was finding it tough to get an internship because of the Victims Law.

I immediately thought I had made a mistake. I did not know Professor Stavisky's politics; perhaps I had just cost myself a great summer job.

"The Victims Law!" he said. "The V-Law! Ha! That is what I think of the V-Law!" He pointed to the back of the door to his office. I turned and looked.

Tacked to the door was a large blow-up of his Non-V Cert, on which was painted a huge red target. In the center of the bulls-eye were four darts that, from the depth of their strike, had been thrown with great force.

I looked closer at the Non-V Cert. It said, "Pyotr Ilyich Stavisky, male, heterosexual, 50% Ashkenazi Jew, 50% Russian Cossack."

"An abomination! The V-Law is an abomination!" he shouted. "That is the reason I have such a wonderful office in the bowels of this building! My politics are not Harvard mainstream! And I am not any kind of Victim!"

He paused, drifting off to follow that thought. "When I got tenure I was a lefty. That was ten years ago. They would never give me tenure now! But they can't take it away! So they stick me in the basement; they hope I will dematerialize!"

"What, exactly, is the job?" I asked, hoping to get back on track.

Stavisky said he had a research grant from the NSA to create a master anti-hacking protocol. It would be something they could bring in like a fire-rescue team if they feared being hacked or if in fact they had been hacked. "Do you know anything about hacking?" he asked.

I decided to give him a bit of my history - excluding the Harvard hack. So I told him about the Stuyvesant hacking competition, about my third and second place finishes, and how I was elected a Lord of Hack senior year. He was very, very interested.

"Do you have your academic transcript?" he asked.

On my cell phone I showed him the transcript showing my record from freshman year of high school through my first semester at Harvard.

"Not many computer courses on here," he said.

"It was mostly extra-curricular," I said.

He liked the answer. "You know," he said, "no other applicant even got half the answers right after thirty minutes. So it seems your little extra-curricular effort paid off - in addition to being a math superstar."

I asked what the job paid. I said I needed enough for a half-share of an apartment with my girl friend and for three meals a day and incidentals.

"We can do that," he said. "And by the way, why wait for summer? Can you start this week?"

12

When I told Sarah, she was ecstatic. Now we could actually live together for a whole summer. We knew we could find a cheap apartment (which we did, in Somerville, one block off Mass. Ave., just across the Cambridge line). And both of us would have interesting jobs.

My parents were thrilled with the summer job. I also told them I thought I had found a roommate for the summer, but would know better in a few weeks. I did not give details; they did not ask further.

With things definitely looking up, Sarah and I settled down for the winter. Even tedious, gray February and muddy March could not get us down.

The work for Stavisky was seriously interesting. Sarah and I were in love; everything was coming up right.

Then we were reminded again what the outside world thought of us as Jews.

It was Passover. Sarah wanted to do the first night Seder at Hillel. I was not eager to sit through a Seder; but after Ari offered to join us, I agreed. He would lighten things up.

"You know, of course, the unwritten story of what happened to Moses on the bank of the Red Sea?" he asked.

I did not, of course, know the unwritten Red Sea story.

"Pharaoh's chariots are bearing down," said Ari. Moses shouts up to Hashem, up there in the pillar of cloud, "O Lord, O Lord, what do I do now?" There is silence - then the answer comes back with a thunderbolt! "File your Environmental Impact Statement!"

Laughing, we neared the Hillel building on Mt. Auburn Street. There we saw a large crowd outside - in fact, two separate crowds.

The first was a group of picketers with anti-Israel signs. The leader was the same tall, full-bearded boy who had glared at us that first night at Mem Church.

I now knew his name - Mahmoud Al -Abb'ss. We had seen his picture twice in The Crimson - once leading a 'seminar' on Israeli war crimes, and once speaking at Boston rally calling for abolition of the State of Israel.

Al-Abb'ss' "nom de guerre" (on his Facebook page) was "Mahmoud Mahmoud". That page ("MahmoudX2") also said he was a Palestinian and a

Harvard senior majoring in Near Eastern Language and Literature. It also alluded to his father's friendship with the Saudi prince who had endowed a professorship in Harvard's Department of Middle East Studies. It did not say who his father was, however.

Mahmoud and his anti-Israel picketers walked in a slow circle on the sidewalk. (After the Mem Church incident I guessed walking in a circle was their thing.)

The second group were Orthodox students, boys with yarmulkes and girls with ankle-length skirts. They stood in a line, without signs, at the edge of the sidewalk, scowling at the picketers.

Each group seemed bent on staring the other to death. (I did not know that Harvard prohibited students from shouting so-called "hate speech" at each other.)

As we passed, Mahmoud just happened to come up to me. As if recognizing me from before, he stopped and stared. I had never seen, up close, such hatred.

"Enjoy your Seder while you can, Jew boy," said Mahmoud. "Your time is coming. You don't know it yet, but I do! All you Jews are about to get yours!'

"Fuck you!" I said, staring back. It wasn't clever – but all I could think of at the time. Then I turned into Hillel.

I don't remember much about that Seder. I was enraged. The Mem Church incident had left me shaken; this one left me pissed, really pissed.

Ari tried to make light of it. He said the black hats – the ultra-Orthodox - were used to taunts of all kinds. These were just Muslims and pro-Muslim fools whose only weapons were placards and words.

I disagreed. Some of the protesters were probably indeed, in Lenin's cliché, "useful idiots". But Mahmoud was different. He was the real thing. And what had he meant by, "You don't know it yet, but I do. All you Jews are about to get yours!"

Sarah was really upset but tried to brush it off. "It's nothing," she said. She tried to joke, citing the line from Harvard's fight song, "Illegitimum non carborundum" - meaning, "don't let the bastards grind you down."

Over the next few days, however, I kept coming back to Mahmoud's words. Something was coming. I knew something was coming - and it would not be good for the Jews.

13

The "something" came, in fact, just two weeks later.

I did not know then how Mahmoud had inside info and how he got it. But two weeks to the day after that Seder, the President announced the "TAgOp Regs".

"AgOp" was short for "Agent of Past Oppression".

"Regs" meant 500 or so pages of regulations published in the Federal Register (the federal government organ for publishing official acts). The "T" was for "temporary."

These "Temporary Agent of Past Oppression Regulations" were supposed to be temporary - only intended, the President said, to last a few years.

When Congress passed the Victims Law, it had directed the Justice Department to determine if any group or groups were responsible for the plight of Victims in America. If it identified such a group, the Justice Department was to propose appropriate remediation or recompense which might be due from that group.

This was a little-known provision in the Victims Law. It had not been highlighted or even mentioned when the Victims Law was rushed through Congress.

After extensive research, said the President, the Justice Department had identified two groups of oppressors - white males and Jews.

White males, the President said, were penalized enough already by being classified as Non-Victims. While their collective guilt was clear and universally accepted, it would be legally complicated to penalize individual males without evidence of identifiable categories of specific oppression.

Jews, however, were different.

The Justice Department had assembled a vast and specific record of acts of oppression by Jews against Victims - going back to the slave trade and before. For example, said the President, it was undisputed historical fact that the "triangle trade" of rum, molasses, and slaves was the brainchild of the Jews.

The Justice Department had also found other "known" categories of Jewish oppression from slavery to the current day.

Among others, noted the President, these included Jewish domination of real estate and banking (resulting in housing and lending exploitation of Victims); Jewish domination of Hollywood and use of the film to perpetuate racial and ethnic stereotypes (citing "Gone With the Wind"); Jewish domination of the professions to the exclusion of Victims; Jewish scientists' culpability for the atomic bomb and then the Rosenbergs' betrayal of nuclear secrets to the Soviet Union; and, more recently, Jewish domination of the internet and technology (such as the corrupting creation of FaceBook).

The Justice Department found, further, that the Jews of Wall Street sabotaged hopes for economic recovery under the Obama presidency - and still continued to suppress the U.S. economy. Jews were the reason, the President said, for the now criminally chronic unemployment.

So it was with deep regret but a clear historical mandate, said the President, that the TAgOp Regs were now adopted to remediate historical wrongs.

I did not read the TAgOp Regs. I read summaries in The New York Times and The Crimson.

The bottom line was that Jews - "Agents of Oppression - would get "negative credits" under the Victims Law. They would be moved to the back of every line - for school and college admissions, for

81

employment, for government contracts, indeed for everything where the government dictated preferences.

To formalize their new status Jews would receive a special "AgOp Certificate" under the Victims Law.

"At least it's not a yellow star," Ari joked. But of course it was no joke.

The New York Times ran a smarmy editorial saying the TAgOp Regs were not anti-Semitic but must be considered in the context of history. It was not as if Jews were being asked to pay monetary reparations. Rather, it was appropriate to ask those who had caused so much oppression to suffer a modest sacrifice as remediation for their historic wrongs.

The Times also said the TAgOp Regs were clearly constitutional because Jews were not being singled out as Jews. Rather, they were part of a defined class who had been guilty of documented misconduct.

The Crimson again ran two editorials, one pro and con.

The "pro" editorial mimicked the Times but also talked about Israel's oppression of the Palestinian people that, if not directly adverse to American Victims, cried out for recompense. The writer said this was a logical corollary of the BDS movement (boycott, disinvestment from Israel, sanctions) promoted by all correct-thinking college faculty and students.

The "con" editorial said that the TAgOp Regs were outrageous. They were the beginning of American Nuremberg Laws - an outrageous assault on constitutional rights by the controlling Democratic Party, which it called the "American Stalinists". This would end tragically, wrote the author.

Muslim organizations were jubilant.

Muslim Americans for a Fair Response (MAFR), the leading jihadist fundraising front (which nonetheless had federal tax-exempt status), praised the government for finally acknowledging the historic crimes of the Jews. "Their modern evils against Palestine are now revealed as only the latest in centuries of calumnies they have inflicted on the civilized world," MAFR said in a press release.

On a whim I googled the MAFR board of directors. One name - Raffiqq Abb'ss - was familiar. When I googled his bio, I discovered why. He was the father of Mahmoud Mahmoud.

I remembered seeing his name before. He advised Middle Eastern countries on the creation of endowed professorships in Islamic Studies at American universities - like the one mentioned on his son's Facebook page.

Mr. Abb'ss was mentioned in a <u>Crimson</u> story last autumn about a major gift to Harvard. Apparently he had been born in the U.S. while his parents were studying here on Fulbright visiting scholarships.

14

Jewish students at Harvard were in shock. Who could have imagined that progressive good works could lead to such a result?

Jews were the good guys, fighters against the enemies of social justice, fighters for oppressed minorities, and (except for a small percentage) Democrats!

How could the Democrats let this happen to one of their oldest and most steadfast constituencies?

A small minority of Harvard Jews applauded the TAgOp Regs, however. They, students and faculty, had been in the forefront of the BDS movement.

"They are the self-hating Jews," Ari said. "In every age there are some. They are fools. They have not read their history; they forget that they will be on the same list for the gas chambers. In fact, they will be at the top of the list. In every revolution the Jewish partisans are always the first to be purged when the revolution succeeds. Just remember Russia."

It took a while before Sarah, Ari, and I received our AgOp Certificates. When they did come, when we each opened our envelope and took out the small, grey plastic card, it was a shock.

Now we knew why the pinprick test and V- and Non-V Certs had identified us as Jews. Our DNA was already in the NSA computers. There was no counterfeiting a false Jewish identity.

"They were obviously planning this from the beginning of the Victims Law," I said to Sarah. "Why else would the V-Cert have identified our Jewish DNA?"

Sarah just shook her head. She always remembered what happened to her grandfather in China. "Not just the Jews," she said. "Also the intellectuals and idealists. But in America the Jews are also the intellectuals and idealists."

Professor Stavisky was beside himself. Apart from his personal and political outrage, he feared they would terminate his NSA grant. He tried to learn as much as he could about the TAgOp Regs.

His first concern, he told me, was who was a Jew. Both his parents were born in the Soviet Union when religion was officially abolished. Only with the end of Communism did his father learn that his mother (Stavisky's grandmother) had been Jewish.

Thus Stavisky's father was a Jew under Jewish law. However, Stavisky's mother was a Cossack; so Stavisky himself, under Jewish law, was not a Jew.

The TAgOp Regs did not apply Jewish law, however. Under the Regs anyone with at least one Jewish grandparent was Jewish, and his or her children were also deemed Jewish.

The TagOp Regs thus captured not just Stavisky but large numbers of Americans who went to Church and believed themselves not Jewish - including many intellectuals who were fashionably anti-Israel.

These people were particularly outraged. They weren't Jewish! How could you be Jewish because of one grandparent! They demanded a change in the TAgOp Regs. Their petitions and lawsuits seeking this change languished at the Justice Department and in the courts.

There was a debate in the blogs and the media as to whether this 'one-grandparent-test' was fair. The mainstream media said it was indeed fair. For centuries even a smaller tinge of black blood had meant you were not white. So why treat Jews differently?

The theory of "disparate impact" was offered in justification of the TAgOp Regs. Developed by late 20th Century African-American intellectuals, "disparate impact" truly came to prominence with the Obama Justice Department. The thesis was that statistics can prove racial discrimination without evidence of actual discrimination.

President Obama's Attorney General, Eric Holder, used "disparate impact" broadly to justify numerous government actions in the name of social justice.

Hence, for example, if a bank charged higher interest rates to members of a statistical minority community, the cause must be racial discrimination per se - regardless of credit scores or financial history.

If a wealthy suburb had no affordable housing, the cause must be racial discrimination per se, regardless of zoning or land prices.

If a public school disproportionately disciplined minority students, the cause must be racial discrimination per se, regardless of the ethnic make-up of the school or actual behavioral problems.

And so on and so forth in all the main areas of human activity.

Apologists for the TAgOp Regs argued, similarly, that "disparate impact" justified the singling out of Jews. They cited, as examples, the disproportionate number of Jews in Hollywood, on Wall Street, in the professions, in real estate, and in hard science (including, perversely, the extraordinary - and vastly disproportionate - number of Jewish Nobel Prize winners). Such documented statistics, argued the apologists, were prima facie evidence of the disparate impact of Jews on Victims.

Similar documented statistics also revealed, said the apologists, "the historic record of oppressive behavior by Jews in the slave trade and in financing the Confederacy." (They omitted to mention the huge role of Arabs and Africans in creating and profiting from the slave trade.)

The "disparate impact" theory was not just a theoretical argument of academicians. It was the conceptual core of the "White Paper" prepared by the Justice Department prior to issuance of the TAgOp Regs. Exhibits to that White Paper included thousands of pages of purported "research" which allegedly documented the disparate impact of Jewish oppression of Victims.

The TAgOp Regs hit my mother the hardest.

A lifelong Democrat, my mother could not understand how or why a Democratic President and Congress had turned on the Jews. Was it not true, she cried, that Jews had been the staunchest supporters of the Democratic Party? "Why? Why? Why?" she kept saying.

If not for Jewish backers and Jewish money, Barack Obama would not have been elected - and re-elected - President.

My father was bitter but not surprised. "Remember Russia," he said. "Lenin and Stalin used their Jews for the Revolution. Without Jews the Soviet Union would never have happened. Then, after the "true" Russians seized control, off with their heads!"

"Trotsky was the poster boy," said my father. "His murder ended Jewish influence in the Party. Stalin and his thugs purged the Jews; and then there was vicious anti-Semitism throughout the Soviet era."

"But this is America!" cried my mother. "Jews were the biggest supporters of the Civil Rights Movement! Jews were the biggest supporters of Barack Obama!"

"I rest my case," said my father. "There has always been anti-Semitism in the black community."

He cited numerous anti-Jew comments by African-American "reverends". An objective observer would not be surprised, he said, based on this particular "historical record", that African-Americans might be quick to dispense with their Jews.

"The Left took Jewish money - they took a lot of Jewish money!" He cited numerous examples of major Jewish donors to the Democratic Party. He laughed. "But the Left now has complete, total, unchallengeable control. They don't need <u>us</u> to get elected anymore. So they can scapegoat us for every ill!"

"I can't believe it!" my mother cried. "This is America!"

"Believe it," said my father. "Remember the Haggadah. 'In every generation they come for us.'" He sighed. "It never changes."

15

None of the "big Jews" in the Democratic Party were forewarned of the TAgOp Regs. They were caught by surprise and outraged. They demanded a meeting with the President.

So the President held a White House meeting with leaders of major Jewish organizations and Hollywood magnates. It was a great photo op - forty or so distinguished Jews all smiling at the President.

The President explained that dire conditions created by Wall Street during the Bush administration had proven intractable. Those conditions did not respond to any known economic cures; new ideas were needed. All intelligent people knew, said the President, of the great contribution of Jews to American society.

Regrettably, however, there was also the historic record of Jewish oppression. The American people could not ignore this, said the President. Since American Jews, as a class, were generally better off than other Americans, the country must ask them to step back in favor of less-favored folks.

And remember, said the President, it was temporary, only temporary. The TAgOp Regs were "temporary". Hopefully things would soon improve, said the President, and the TAgOp Regs could be ended.

The President ended the meeting by saying that temporary Regs <u>now</u> would avoid tougher measures that an angry citizenry, knowing the Jewish record, might demand <u>later</u> if economic conditions got worse.

Afterwards, in their media interviews, the attendees were divided. Some, still good Democrats - defying all logic - accepted the President's line.

Others, however, including five rabbis from the largest Reform congregations, said the whole thing was a charade. The "temporary" regulations would become permanent. The dire economic conditions were not caused by the Bush administration but by the non-recovery since 2009, and now by the stifling effect of the Victims Law. The Victims Law was crushing growth and opportunity throughout the U.S, they said.

The five rabbis announced that they were leaving the Democratic Party and urged their congregations to follow them.

One of the rabbis, David Cohnen, the leader of a major big-city congregation, followed up with an Op Ed in <u>The Wall Street Journal</u>. "We have seen this coming for years but did nothing" he wrote."Anti-Semitism on American campuses has been virulent. Yet the BDS

Israel movement has been just theater scrim, a mask for the vicious Jew-hatred of the Left and of radical Islam."

"Remember," he wrote, "when Ed Koch abandoned the Democrats in 2010 to support a Republican for Congress - he was protesting President Obama's anti-Israel policies. Then the Party forced him to recant before the 2012 presidential election. Later Koch said he recanted because he expected Obama to win and going along would be better for Israel. He knew he was wrong. He was bitter about the 2012 Democratic Convention: "Nobody has adequately explained to me," Koch said, "how the boos for God and Israel were louder than the cheers. How can that be?"

Rabbi Cohnen concluded with a call to arms. "We know now 'how that can be' - how the 2012 Convention could have been anti-Semitic. We have seen it coming but have chosen blinders! We must take off our blinders and fight for survival! Never again!"

Another of the five rabbis, Moses Smith, added a postscript. He said that Democratic anti-Semitism became patently obvious under the Obama Administration - but American Jews took great pains not to see it.

Rabbi Smith noted, first, the Obama Administration's curiously accommodating policies toward Iran, and the President's refusal to use the word

"Islamic" in any context of Islamic terrorism, even the ISIS scourge.

In 2011, Rabbi Smith wrote, President Obama directed a shift from the U.S policy of supporting stability in the Middle East to supporting, instead, Islamist political movements. President Obama gave much unpublicized aid to the Muslim Brotherhood, the grandfather of modern jihadist organizations, and continued to back its leader Mohamed Morsi even after the Egyptian people overthrew the dictatorship of the Brotherhood.

Later, in the 2014 Hamas rocket war against Israel, the Obama bias was even more obvious. With Saudi Arabia and Egypt supporting the Israelis, Secretary Kerry still pushed a "peace plan" proposed by Hamas and its backers, Qatar and Turkey, which would have rewarded Hamas aggression. The Obama Administration, now open in its hostility towards Israel, then cut off weapons shipments to Israel while continuing to send millions to the Palestinians. President Obama later chided Israel at the U.N. for "not trying hard enough" for peace.

Finally, of course, there was President Obama's shunning of Prime Minister Netanyahu, and the boycott by Congressional Democrats, when Netanyahu addressed Congress in March, 2015.

"What does it take for American Jews to see reality?" Rabbi Smith concluded. "How long can they deliberately look away?"

Shortly after the White House meeting two Democratic Senators withdrew from the party and became independents. They were excoriated by party leadership but cheered in their home states (one in the South and one in the West). Their withdrawal did not, however, tip voting power in the Senate.

No Republican in Congress had been told in advance that Justice would issue the TAgOp Regs.

The powerless Republicans excoriated the Democrats. They charged that the TagOp Regs were the worst abuse of government power in American history.

Richard Nixon would not have resigned, they said, if many Republicans had not put good of country ahead of saving their party and said, "No". And Watergate, after all, was only a bungled burglary.

By contrast, since the Clinton impeachment, no leading Democrat had stood up and said no to any party wrongdoing. (The Republicans cited, among others in a long list of scandals, Fast and Furious, Benghazi, and the IRS targeting of conservatives.)

Where were the good Democrats? Would any Democrat object? How, now, could Democrats not stand up and say, "No!"?

Republicans organized a 24-hour vigil on the steps of the Capitol and in state capitals across the country. Hundreds of thousands, carrying candles, sang and prayed through the night. But a vigil and candles could not create votes.

The Anti-Defamation League took a full-page, back-page ad in <u>The New York Times</u> to dispute the factual inaccuracies in the Administration's purported "historic research". The ad refuted, point-by-point, each key premise offered by the "disparate impact" theorists of the Justice Department.

Among the most blatant "untruths", said the ADL, was that Jews started and were deeply involved in the African slave trade. To the contrary, the slave trade dated back at least to the 11th Century when there was documented evidence of major slave trafficking among Arab slavers and African tribes. Jews were never the prime movers or masterminds of the slave trade.

In contrast, predictably, applause for the TagOp Regs continued from the media organs of the Left, from Muslim organizations, and from university campuses.

The university campuses were no surprise, of course, because for years the hard Left had dominated faculty lounges and brainwashed the students. Indeed, the BDS Israel movement started in the universities, with help from Protestant church groups and world peace activists.[†]

The Harvard campus was no exception. Many students and faculty (including self-hating Jews) cheered the TAgOp Regs. The supporters of TAgOp organized a two-hour program in Sanders Theater at which students and faculty read aloud the entire text of the Regs. One of the organizers was Mahmoud Mahmoud.

[†] In contrast, evangelical Christians, avid supporters of Israel, detested the BDS movement and vehemently protested the TAgOp Regs with numerous demonstrations, prayer meetings, and door-to-door protests.

16

Advancing technology now rubbed salt in our wounds. The original NSA pinprick test required you to go to a clinic or a doctor's office – like the day we went to HHS. Now hand-held DNA devices were distributed to schools, colleges, employers, and government agencies.

The hand-held devices looked like small smartphones with a tiny claw. The claw did not draw blood, which would have been unhygienic. Instead, with a simple rub on your skin, the claw absorbed a DNA sample. Five seconds later your V, or Non-V, or AgOp status showed on the display.

In no time the claw was everywhere. Officially termed a "V-Status Tester", it was soon just called the "Jew Catcher". The Justice Department said it was to promote "ease of administration" so a plastic card would no longer be necessary.

There was no place to hide.

Sarah, Ari, and I were stunned. During freshman year we had each begun to make friends among our fellow students. Now we were suspicious of anyone who was not Jewish.

To Stavisky's amazement, the NSA did not cancel his contract. "We're lucky. But I'm not surprised," he said. "Government is so screwed it will take them a while to figure out who I am. Also, at least right now, the Jew Rules only apply to <u>new</u> contracts; so maybe they do not look backward."

Stavisky made a new dartboard from a copy of his AgOp Certificate. There were seven darts stuck deep on that board in the back of his door.

17

I continued at Stavisky's lab four afternoons a week, with added evening time when I could, exploring the NSA's security protocols.

Government may have been inefficient, but hackers weren't. As soon as experts could make new security fences, hackers could scale them. This was the true World War III.

All over the world computer geeks - at corporations, governments, and consulting firms – worked feverishly on new security protections. Arrayed against them - from attics, offices, or government spy-centers - were the enemy geeks, the warriors of the web.

Any security wall the human mind could devise the human mind could also un-devise. This was a silent war without public proclamations, borders, or limits. The public knew nothing. Yet the battles, if bloodless, were as cosmic and potentially destructive as any in history.

Stavisky's contract was, in part, to create an early warning system to catch enemy hacks at the door, at the first point of entry. For this contract he had received the highest NSA security clearance.

At the outset he had to get me a similar clearance to work on the project. Surprisingly, this took only one day. When I asked why so quick, he said, "They trust me."

Thus in incredibly short time I had access to NSA files which were available to only a handful of the highest officials and geeks of NSA. Apparently my AgOp Cert was not, when it arrived later, a problem. "They hate us," Stavisky said, "but they are not stupid. They know where the brains are."

And that is how I found myself playing in the vast fields of NSA meta-data.

After the Snowden leaks of 2013, after the publicity and Congressional hearings, the Obama administration promised to put limits on the NSA's data collection. Thus the public now believed that NSA spying was reduced, that there was less spying on private lives.

The contrary was true.

Instead of shrinking and restricting, the NSA expanded and broadened. Indeed, with technology advancing exponentially, the NSA's range and ability to spy had increased by a factor of 20. To cover its tracks the NSA simply adopted more intensely secret protocols.

Which is where Stavisky - and his new assistant - came in. It was our job to test these secret protocols, to hide the NSA prying from the world's cleverest spies.

The first time I entered the NSA data sectors I literally stopped breathing.

The scale was beyond anything I could imagine, even in my most extreme hacker mode. There were beyond billions of information bits from every sector of digital human activity. Every cell-phone call, every email, every web-search, every internet transaction - it was all there.

Just for the hell of it, I dug for my own file. And there it was - going back to the beginning. Every stupid email I had ever sent. Every web search I had ever made. They even had files from my first Stuyvesant hack! (They did not have the later hacks because I had used more secure remote email addresses, which was reassuring.)

I thought I would be sick. I logged out, stood up, and walked out of the lab just as Stavisky was entering.

"What's the matter?" he asked. "You look sick."

I told him what I had just seen.

"You'll get used to it," he said. "It's like the first time a med student examines a cadaver. It's scary and bloody and you want to throw up. But then, like everything else, you become calloused."

He was right. I soon became calloused.

Within the NSA data fields we hunted spies and attackers. Some were easy to find. They were clumsy bunglers (albeit clever enough to get into the NSA) whose tracks, like deer prints in snow, were clear right away. Such bunglers never made it past the front door.

A larger number made it to the front door and just inside, but were then caught in our digital rabbit traps.

The real threats were only a handful, but with great resources and greater ingenuity. These were the ninjas of the web. (We did, indeed, call them "ninjas").

They operated from greynets of their own creation, in alternate universes, outside the borders of the internet. From these remote places, deep in the undiscovered regions of the web, they launched stealth attacks on victims who often did not know they had been hacked until long after - when they discovered that national or industrial secrets, if not large sums of money, had gone missing.

Stavisky's project had two main parts – first, to detect the different kinds of attacks and, second, to create programs to stop them.

Before I could be useful, Stavisky told me, I had to learn the NSA file categories. I had to understand the conceptual structures. Which, as fate would have it, led me to the Victim files.

The Victim files were completely separate from all other NSA metadata. This was because the Victim files were a <u>management</u> category for NSA, Stavisky said, meaning an <u>administrative</u> responsibility - very different from metadata collection, which was just spying.

The servers for the Victim files were not in Washington; they were scattered in four locations around the U.S. - upstate New York, Mississippi, Idaho, and West Virginia.

Why four? I asked Staviky. For redundancy, he answered. Then he added, "Given the typical government planning process, those four took several years to set up. So they must have been created <u>before</u> Congress passed the Victims Law. Someone has been planning this whole Victim thing for a long time." He shuddered. "And probably, also, the Jew Rules!"

I had expected that the Victim files would just include name, address, and V or Non-V or AgOp status. Instead there was more.

Each file showed the person's racial or ethnic mixture by percentage breakdown with related coding. There were also names of the person's parents and grandparents (and links to their files).[‡]

Some files had little boxes with question marks and the notation, "pending verification". Others, weirdly, had little boxes with from one to three plus or minus signs.

I understood "pending verification", ominous as that might be. I did not understand the plus or minus signs. What did they mean? And who made them? Sooner or later I expected that I might find the answers to these questions.

There were separate "AgOp" files for Jews - outside all other Victim files. Although every Jew did have a Victim file, it was a directional sign. When you clicked the Victim file for, say, "Julie Goldberg," you were immediately directed to Julie's AgOp File.

When I told Stavisky about the separate Jew files, he slammed his desk and cursed in Russian. "That was

---

[‡] There were many typos and misspellings, probably because of input from the original V-Law filings.

not just set up!" he said. "The TAgOp Regs were only announced six weeks ago. How could an entire separate file system for Jews have been created in just six weeks?"

Stavisky was right, of course.

I searched the AgOp files to learn when they had been created. They dated, in fact, to the original creation of the Victim Files.

The AgOp file structure was contemporaneous with the programming for the Victim Files. In the earliest Victim file structure was a program that transferred to AgOp files the entire Victim or non-Victim file on a person with <u>any</u> Jewish DNA.

I checked the AgOp files to see if they had the same 'plus' or 'minus' notes as the Victim files. They did.

The Jew Files, as Stavisky quickly named them, were identical to Victim and non-Victim files. They had the same sub-files on ancestors, the same percentage breakdowns, the same "pending verification" - <u>and</u> the same pluses or minuses.

I asked Stavisky if he knew who had created the NSA files. He did not know. He said he had done some sleuthing on that question, but without success. The answer, he said - if we could find it - might give us the real backstory on the Victims Law. And so we began to dig.

18

Spring came to Cambridge. Even the AgOp crap could not diminish the rush we felt when released from winter's gray doom.

Sarah and I resumed our afternoon math sessions by the Weeks Bridge. Even though we now had the summer apartment (it started May 1st!) and could be together at will, we still loved to sit on the grass near the river and do math problems. It was a special ritual, an important part of our brief history together.

There were increasing reminders, however, of our new AgOp status.

The first shock came when, after our V- check while buying tickets for the Boston Pops, the box office girl said there were no orchestra seats. She must be mistaken, I said. I pointed to the digital seating chart that showed a number of open orchestra seats. "Sorry," she apologized. "Those seats aren't available for your...category. For you, there are only seats in the second balcony."

We were so stunned that we bought the balcony seats. Then, leaving the box office, we looked at each other and felt ashamed. I tore up the tickets, which had not been cheap and, saying nothing, we walked off down Huntington Avenue.

More and more, now, we were reminded that we were Jews.

Each time we had a V-check - required at airports, libraries, for online ticket purchases of all kinds, even at some restaurants - there were subtle and not-so-subtle messages. These ranged from a slight averted glance by the checker, to getting second-class status, to being told there was no room at the inn.

And that was before Part Two of the TAgOp Regs.

Part One (which had not been called "Part One" until the issuance of Part Two) had classified Jews as TAgOps and demoted us. Part One "just" provided that AgOps - meaning Jews - would go to the back of the line in all classifications relevant to V-status.

When the Justice Department issued Part Two, it formally renamed the original TAgOp Regs, "Part One."

Part Two was crushing. Part Two specified the special types of treatment Jews would receive as remediation for our historic sins.

There were three "Sections" to Part Two -Section One, employment rules, including professional licensing;

110

Section Two, school and university admissions; and Section Three, government contracting and financial or research grants. (The travel, property-ownership, and other restrictions would come later.)

The stated premise of the V- Law, when passed by Congress, was that Victims would take a step forward; all others would come next. There would be positive preferences but no negatives. No one would step back.

Part One of the TAgOp Regs changed that, of course. Under Part One Jews went to the back of the bus.

Part Two then threw us mostly off the bus.

AgOps (meaning you-know-who) would now be restricted by numerical quotas in all three Sections - and very small quotas indeed. We could now have no more than a small fraction of the last seats on the bus.

Thus, for example, Jews were now limited to no more than five percent of applicants for a bar exam or medical board. No more than five percent of admittees to any college could be Jews. Jews could not own more than five percent of any firm applying for a federal, state, or local government contract. No more than five percent of any government financial grant program could be allocated to Jews or firms controlled by Jews.

Part Two did not say "Jews", of course. It said "AgOps" - but I hate that term and will use it as little as possible.

My mother was the first person in our family to be stung by Part Two. She had twenty-six years as a New York City public school teacher and could have retired long before; yet she continued working because she loved teaching. ("What am I, crazy?" she would joke. "Of course – but you knew that already!").

One month after the Justice Department issued Part Two, she received a pink slip from the City. This "Status-Change Notice" said her termination was "for legal compliance". Outraged, she called the Board of Ed and asked, "What the hell does that mean?" No one could say.

After finally reaching an old friend in the Board of Ed main office, she was told, "It's the TAgOp thing. Part Two requires us to cut the number of AgOps. So, it's easiest to start with people who are past retirement age. Which, unfortunately, is you."

Losing her job changed my mother's life.

Being a teacher had been her identity. It was not just a job. Of course, being a Democrat had also been her identity. Now, having lost the two poles of her being, she was dazed. She swung between rage and

112

despair. She did not know what to do. Every morning, facing a hopeless future, she went to Central Park and walked in a fog around the Park roadway.

It was as if she had disappeared from our lives. My father did not know what to do. Each morning he called to ask me for advice. He was also worried about his own City job. But, he joked wryly, "How can they cut Jews from the City Law Department? They'll have no one left." (He proved wrong, of course).

My mother was not alone. Soon we heard more such stories. Schools, universities, government agencies, large corporations, all started trimming their Jews.

When asked at a press conference about widespread firings of Jews, the President denied any knowledge.

The President said such rumors of firings could not be believed. They were very likely fabrications of Right-wing extremists.

It was not the purpose of Part Two to cause firings, said the President, but rather to ensure that AgOps contributed fairly to offset the historic pain of Victims. Certainly, the President insisted, this did not mean that AgOps should be fired. It meant, rather, that AgOpsOps should be reminded of the national need for social justice.

Besides, the President said, "I have been assured that this will not affect more than a sampling of people - and, remember, it's only temporary."

Then we heard personal reports - not rumors - of actual firings at Harvard.

Ari's Jewish section assistant in Bio Chem was replaced with an African-American. The untenured Jewish professor in Sarah's Core American History course (Revolution to Civil War) took a sudden leave of absence. The new professor was a Latina woman whose field was gender discrimination.

To its credit, The Crimson got on this story. It ran a number of pieces listing firings of AgOp faculty. Then, however, the stories stopped.

"There are a lot of Yids on that paper," Ari said. "I guess they got to them. You - Jew -do you want to stay at Harvard? So much for journalistic integrity."

Ari was wrong about one editor, however. Ephraim Goldstein, the Editorial Chairman, did resign. He tweeted friends that the Harvard administration had issued an ultimatum - stop the Jew firing stories or be suspended or worse[§]. Crimson executives debated the

---

[§] We confirmed later that this was true. The President of The Crimson had been told directly by a senior Dean that if the stories

114

matter and decided it was better to avoid suspension in the hope, later, to write the truth.

Goldstein said he could not stomach surrender and so resigned. "They don't see what's coming," he wrote.

A new student organization (with both Jews and non-Jews) - "Repeal the Regs" or "RTR" - applied for a permit to hold a daylong demonstration on the Widener steps. The University denied the application.

Undaunted, RTR began a weekly march (every Sunday) around the perimeter sidewalks of The Yard. Many non-Jews walked with them. Each week the number of marchers grew. Eventually they were a solid line of humanity all the way around The Yard.

The RTR movement quickly spread to other cities. Sundays became the quiet protest day throughout the United States.

---

did not stop, the authors faced suspension or even expulsion. There was nothing in writing, of course.

19

Amid, and despite, all these events, ordinary life continued. Soon it was exam time again.

Once more I got all A's - even though I had to check a special box on the exam book indicating my Victim status -"AgOp" - Jew.

With school out and summer starting, Sarah and I settled in to our small apartment. Nothing - not the events of the world or the AgOp crap - could diminish our happiness. Of course, you will say, we were playing at domesticity - but it was great play.

Days we went to our jobs. Nights we shopped for groceries and made dinner at the small kitchen table, usually with a glass of wine. Then we made love - or, tired from the workday, just lay in bed and held each other.

Weekends we explored Boston or listened to outdoor concerts (where seats on the ground were not yet rationed for Jews).

I was learning more each day how special Sarah was. Among other things, she had her daily and weekly rituals that I came to love, from the way she brushed her hair in the morning to the lighting of Shabbos candles on Friday night.

Sarah told me she had lit the candles with her mother from the time she was a little girl. While Reform in observance, her mother was quite spiritual and had wanted to instill in her respect for the simple rituals of Jewish life. Lighting candles also reminded her, Sarah said, of the good times she had spent with her mother and father.

So every Friday night Sarah lit the candles, and we also said Kiddush over wine and the blessing for breaking bread.

Sarah loved her job. She discovered that most actuaries were very smart, if not charismatic. Her employer was a mid-size firm, and the people were nice. She had never known how many businesses and professions needed actuarial or statistical calculations. "So many firms need math analysis," she said.

Sarah guessed most of her co-workers assumed she was Chinese. Would they have treated her differently if they knew her DNA?

All over the country Jews reported subtle and not-so-subtle differences in workplace treatment, even from colleagues they had known for years. "As if we are aliens," one Beth Zwartz posted on Facebook.

I continued to roam the NSA data fields with Stavisky. I quickly became skilled at detecting intruders. That was the easy part, Stavisky said.

"First catch, then destroy!" was Stavisky's mantra. My next task was to write a catch-and-destroy program to do that automatically.

Even with my extensive hacking history, my first attempts to create that program were crude. Hacking into a system was one thing; creating an entire catch-and-destroy program was another.

"Think of it as building a castle wall," said Stavisky. "That is the first step. Then, once you have built the wall, how do you catch invaders while they try to climb it?"

He chewed on his pipe. "And, after you catch them - and before you destroy them - you must learn where they live and send back the plague!"

The plague! How to create the computer equivalent of the plague?

It was far easier said than done. But I was learning from a master.

Soon I was able to build my castle walls. That was the simplest step.

Catching the intruders at their first contact was more difficult. After that, it would be a while, I thought, before I mastered the finding-where-they-live and send-back-the-plague parts.

Yet the "while" came sooner than expected.

I remember that it was a June afternoon. I was walking back to the apartment after a complete dead-end day. Two weeks after building the castle walls, I had finally created a brilliant program to catch intruders. But I was still unable to track them back to their bases and send the plague.

As I was waiting to cross Mass. Ave., it hit me. I figured out the math to "walk the past" of an intruder back to his or her base. And, being able to walk the past, I could then administer the plague. There it was!

I let out a yell and pumped my right fist into the air. An old woman nearby stared as if she might call the police. I smiled at her and said it was nothing to worry about - just good news. I rushed back to the lab to try it out.

Of course the math worked. Of course the program worked.

It was a perfect coincidence that, as I was finishing the program, I detected a would-be invader hacking in - from Iceland, of all places. I let him take a few steps into the files, then pulled the trigger. He was ejected from the files and pushed back to Iceland. With him went my new virus, which then infected his home files and programs, as well as any computers contacting him. The plague had come to Iceland.

I called it the "plague virus" - what else?

Stavisky was overjoyed. He loved the name, "plague virus". But then he said something troubling. "We should keep this to ourselves."

I stared at him.

"I am not sure how long we have," he said. He told me he had received two weird phone calls in the past two days. Both were from his NSA Program Director, the man who administered his grant.

On the first call the PD said he was just checking in, just wanting to see how things were going. "How far along are you on the intruder program?" asked the PD.

Stavisky responded that he was close to the answer, but as yet not quite there. Why was the PD asking? After all, Stavisky said, he had four months left on his schedule for delivery of the program. "Oh, just checking in," had been the PD's answer.

Two days later, on the next call, the PD asked if Stavisky could send him an interim copy of the new program, even if unfinished. Why did the PD want an unfinished program? Stavisky asked. "Oh, you know, they are pushing me to get progress evidence of what you are doing," said the PD.

"Something's up," Stavisky told me. "I think they have finally connected the dots. They have realized that we are Jews – now they see the risk in us roaming through the NSA files!"

So we did not tell them about the plague virus. In fact, as luck would have it, although I had told Stavisky about the plague virus, I had not gotten around to showing him the programming.

Stavisky did send them a bastardized version of his own detection program. However, among several secret defects, it did not detect real intruders, only phantom ones; and, of course, it did not have the 'track back' and 'plague' parts of my programs.

Because Stavisky's paranoia got to me, I did two things.

First, I made copies of my track back and plague programs, which I put on two zip drives. Then I rented safe deposit boxes at two Boston banks in each of which

I left one zip drive. I also created a new secret email account in the greynet and left a copy there.

Second, I created a 'back-door key' – a secret code that allowed me to sneak through the very walls and intruder searches I had created. With this key I myself could become an almost-invisible intruder sneaking into the NSA files from outside. I would be the 21st Century invisible man.

Sure enough, one week later, without notice from his PD, Stavisky was locked out of the NSA files. He used each of his three different passwords - no luck.

Then the same happened to me. In all cases, after we typed our usual entry codes and passwords, the computer said simply, "Not recognized."

When Stavisky called to ask why, the PD took a day to call back. When the PD finally did respond, he denied knowledge of what had happened. He told Staviskly he would check and get back to him.

Two days later the PD called back. "I'm sorry," he said, "but the NSA has decided to take a new approach to this whole subject. So we won't need you to continue. But don't worry about your funding. The balance will be paid on schedule. It's not your fault. We are just rethinking the whole process. So we are terminating you for convenience." He did not say it was because we were Yids.

20

So Stavisky and I were terminated for convenience. This, we found, was now happening to many Jews who did business with the federal government.

I thought Sarah would be shocked. She was not. She was tougher and more realistic than her Chinese loveliness would suggest.

"This is still the beginning," she said. "History has too many wretched lessons like this. Believe me, I know from China. Each revolution is the same. It gets more and more radical, then ends in iron tyranny. But that can take years. Meanwhile we Jews live in the "now" - and "now" is always bad for us!"

Her face was cold. "One thing is always the same. They always come for the Jews - either early, like the start of the Crusades, or later, when the revolution succeeds, and the Party purges its Jewish brains!"

She paused. "And, of course, they always take our money! The Jews of America had better empty their bank accounts!"

In my case, of course, there was not much to empty.

Stavisky told me he would pay me through the summer and beyond, as long he received his grant payments. He asked that we still get together at least once a week just to talk. He said there were few people he could really talk to, and I was one.

I agreed readily and thus, every Wednesday afternoon, went to his office to chat about everything from complex computer theory to the latest rumors of Justice Department repression of Jews.

I waited several weeks until the shock of the NSA termination wore off. Then I decided to see if my back-door key still worked – was I still the invisible man?

One morning after Sarah went off to work, I hacked into the NSA files. My back-door key worked, of course. Why should I have doubted? Not only did it work, but I was invisible.

I was proud of my invisibility. Needless to say, to trap intruders I had had to figure out how and why a ninja hacker might try to become invisible. In that way I had created my own invisibility code.

Someday some new "me" at the NSA would catch me; but not for a while, especially if they were firing the Jews. I was invisible.

So I roamed again, and at will, through the NSA's AgOp files. There they were, all the Jews of America, adults and children, with all their pluses and minuses.

Stavisky and I had not yet figured out the meaning of the pluses and minuses, nor who created them. We discussed this at some length. Figuring out the meaning of the pluses and minuses was my next task.

I decided to lie in wait until I found someone - some NSA person - making a plus or minus entry in a Jew file. Surprisingly, it took no longer than getting up for a fresh cup of black coffee.

When I sat back down, coffee in hand, a file was being changed, right before my eyes.

At the start the file had no pluses or minuses; then, as I watched, some NSA hand inserted one minus in the file of Samuel Klein of Cleveland, Ohio.

I was easily able to track the NSA person who had made the change. He or she was located in something called the "AO Directorate".

With that information I found a whole lot more. Officially, the AO Directorate did not exist.

It was not listed in any U.S. government publications or websites. It had not been written about in any publications. No federal official had ever mentioned it in Congressional hearings or departmental briefings. It was not the subject of any media stories.

Unofficially, however, the AO Directorate was very real. It was located in an old office building in downtown Boston, of all places.

After finding the address, I looked at the building on Google Maps. It was nondescript, located in the midst of a bunch of other old gray Boston buildings. People coming and going would not be noticed. In contrast, I thought, if they had put it in a suburban mall, people would have noticed.

I wanted to visit the building and check out the tenant directory. I wondered what they called themselves - probably "Acme Finance Company" or some other cliché name. I decided, however, not to visit the building. NSA cameras would check out every person entering or leaving the building - and probably those passing on the street.

I did not want to show up on any NSA scan. Given my NSA clearance and recent termination, that might immediately set off alarms.

I had to content myself with a virtual look at the building directory. Since I knew the NSA would also scan everyone checking out the building's directory, I made an avatar on the greynet who did that work from a web address in Nebraska.

The building had nine tenants, all with generic names. This meant, I guessed, that the AO Directorate occupied the whole building. I destroyed my avatar and all evidence of the Nebraska web address.

Who ran the AO Directorate? That took two weeks of digging.

The NSA had created the AO Directorate to comply with a secret Executive Order of the President. That order - E.O. 2017/43 - coincided with the President's signing of the Victims Law. This was the smoking gun.

Confirming what we already knew, the Administration had been planning its "temporary" Jewish solution from the very beginning!

The five members of the AO Directorate were appointed directly by the President. Four names I did not recognize. But the fifth I now knew well - Raffiqq Abb'ss. How had he come to be appointed to a secret, anti-Jewish federal government agency?

21

Pre-occupied as I was with the NSA files and the AO Directorate, I had given no thought to Fall classes. Then, in early August, a bomb exploded. I received notice that I must defer the Fall semester.

The notice was an email from the Dean of the College. It gave no reason but said that I should contact an assistant dean (phone number included) with any questions. I called immediately.

The assistant dean was wimpy and apologetic. Clearly following a 'talking points' script, he said new federal rules required Harvard to make room for Victims who were transferring from other schools. To comply, he said, the College had reviewed the status of all non-Victims (especially Jews! I thought) in low-priority concentrations. I was on the list, he said, since math was not a high priority. I must defer until the next semester.

"What then?" I asked. "How can you move me out for a Victim now and then have room in winter to move me back in?"

That question was not in his script. He was flustered. "I'm sure they have thought of that," he said.

"They would not ask you to defer for only one semester if they had not figured that out."

I wondered who "they" were but did not bother to ask.

Sarah was not deferred, probably because she was a woman (even if Jewish). Nor was Ari. Pre-med must still be a priority, especially given the now-serious doctor shortages under ObamaCare.

My parents were terribly upset. This was another in the 'death of a thousand cuts' they were experiencing. My news did, however, have one good effect. It jolted my thin, grey-haired mother out of her depression.

Once she had been an activist for the Democratic Left. Now she took up arms for her people.

She was outraged. She was energized.

Through the web she began to contact other angry New York Jews. She started her own blog, "What Is To Be Done?" under the name "Hadassah AgOp".

Hadassah AgOp quickly became a chronicler of bad things happening to Jews under Part Two.

At first she reported rumors she heard; then people began to send their stories to her. (She never mentioned names unless the victim wanted his or her name disclosed.)

In no time the trickle of stories became a flood. Throughout New York and the U.S., Jews began to lose their public and private jobs; Jews were barred from applying to college; after three years of school, Jewish law students were stopped from taking bar exams; Jewish firms were disqualified from bidding for contracts.

Hadassah AgOp's reports were simple and factual. She devoted a single short paragraph to each story. The cumulative effect was devastating. She was soon getting over 100,000 readers each day.

Every morning, after she finished her newest posts, she cried. Nothing could help her anger.

My father was angry also, but indecisive. What could anyone do? The Obama presidency had neutered Congress through Executive Orders that vastly increased the executive power. The courts then turned away challenges to those orders on procedural grounds or on plaintiffs' lack of standing to sue.

My father despaired. He was a lawyer trained in old school jurisprudence. This was not the law he had learned at Columbia.

And then, of course, he lost his job.

It was the same New York City pink slip my mother had received. Since my father was now well past voluntary retirement age, it said, he was being terminated for "legal compliance."

He stormed into the office of his boss, the City's Corporation Counsel, an African-American whom he had known for years. "What can I say?" was the answer to his question. "It's Part Two of the AgOp Regs. We have to reduce AgOp attorneys to no more than five percent."

The Corp. Counsel was genuinely distraught. "Believe me, we want to hurt as few people as possible. So we decided to cut first from people like you who are past retirement age and can collect a pension. Unfortunately, there are others who can't yet collect their pension." He shook his head sadly. "You know I don't believe in this. But it's the law. What can I say?"

So, thirty days later, after 41 years practicing law for the City of New York, my father was on the street.

Since my parents were collecting their pensions (cancelling pensions for AgOps would only come later), they did not suffer financially. Also, my father had received a nice inheritance from my grandfather, a garment manufacturer, which my father had increased through cautious investing. (Perversely, because this freed him financially from the need to practice law, he spent his entire career in the City Law Department, which paid much less than private law practice.)

Since my grandfather's fund also paid for Harvard, my father's firing would not stop me from returning to the College – if my deferral was not permanent.

22

Without Harvard housing I needed a place to live if I wanted to say in Cambridge.

As a result of my deferral, I had lost my place in Lowell House - to which I had been assigned through House selection. (Upper classmen lived in the Harvard "Houses", each a mini-campus, after leaving the freshman dorms in the Yard.) Lowell was one of the great Georgian Houses below Mount Auburn Street and near the Charles River.

Since we had applied together, and since she was not deferred, Sarah got a single in Lowell.

Then I had a stroke of great luck.

Our summer apartment was in a small building owned by an elderly Jewish couple, Mr. and Mrs. Rosensteil. While we did not know them well, we paid our rent promptly and tried to be good tenants.

A few days after my phone call with the assistant dean, I met Mr. Rosensteil in the building lobby. When he asked how I was, instead of a perfunctory answer, I told him the whole story - that I had been deferred, what an outrage it was, etc.

David Rosensteil was a modest man in his sixties with gray hair and sloped shoulders, who you might see browsing in a bookstore or a supermarket aisle. He listened sadly, then said that he and Mrs. Rosensteil had been following the whole TAgOp thing - how could he not? They were outraged beyond words, he said. Then we parted.

Three weeks later, as I considered my lack of options for the fall, Mr. Rosensteil knocked on my door. He asked where I would stay during my deferral. I said I did not know - that I could not live at Harvard but wanted to stay in Cambridge. "Ah hah!" he laughed. "Do I have a deal for you!"

Then Mr. Rosensteil made one of the kindest proposals I had ever received. He asked how much I could pay. I told him I could pay about half the rent Sarah and I were paying but would have to speak with my parents. He said he and Mrs. Rosensteil wanted to help me out, that they knew I was a brilliant kid - and, drum roll, they would accept whatever I could pay. It was a way for them to protest the TAgOp Regs.

My parents agreed immediately, of course. Now I had a roof over my head for the indefinite future!

An idle mind, they say, is the devil's workshop. Well, now I had a very idle mind, and I could focus entirely on NSA metadata and the AgOp files. I did not know what I might find; but I sensed there was something I must do.

I had not told Stavisky about my back-door key into the NSA; nor did I intend to. It was not, of course, that I did not trust him (although I decided that "trust no one" was now my guiding principle).

I had become very fond of the tall, crotchety Cossack-Jew. I did not want to get him into trouble because of involvement with me if I got caught.

So every morning, after skimming the Crimson and scanning the web, I poured my second cup of Java and snuck through the back door of the NSA.

At first, because I did not have any goal or plan, I did random searches, including checking on people I knew. After a few days of this, I happened to look at my mother's file. Something had changed.

Earlier, when I first looked at her file, shortly after Justice announced Part Two, the file was plain vanilla, no pluses or minuses. Later, when she lost her job, this did not change. However, as soon as Hadassah AgOp became the feisty blogger, three minuses appeared. Someone - or something - had observed her new activism. That someone or something, I concluded, must be a computer.

Unless the AO Directorate had thousands of people reviewing untold numbers of internet pages each day, only a computer could do this – and with vastly greater reach.

I looked with new interest through the NSA files and saw many more pluses or minuses than Stavisky and I had seen at the outset. Now there were not just hundreds or thousands but millions. The watcher could only be a computer; and I had to find and watch the watcher.

It did not take me long. I did not, of course, use my mother's file as the guinea pig. I did not want anyone - or any machine - tracing my steps back to her. Rather, I picked a random file on a Victim - an African-American, not an AgOp. I was intrigued, anyway, as to why a Victim might also get minuses.

I was able to backtrack from a 'minus' in this woman's file to not one, but a series of programs which led, in turn, to a master program of great sophistication. I started calling this program simply the "Watcher". I would have called it the "Jew Watcher" except that it watched <u>everyone.</u>

The Watcher scanned everyone, all the time. It had three categories of action for those it watched. For random action without clear impact under the Victims Law, it did nothing. For actions adverse to the Victims

Law, it entered a minus. For actions supporting the Victims Law, it entered a plus.

There was also, I discovered, a Justice Department website for anonymous tips on individuals who were speaking or acting in a manner "hostile" to the Victims Law. The Watcher harvested these tips, of which there were now thousands, deemed them 'actions adverse', and entered a minus in the file of the reported offender.

What happened after the Watcher entered a minus or a plus, I did not yet know. I expected, however, that a minus was not good news.

The next breakthrough came as I was again sitting over morning coffee looking out at traffic on Mass. Avenue. (Our little apartment was on the second floor with a view towards Mass. Avenue.)

Sarah had gone off to class. (I forgot to mention that she continued to stay in the apartment even though she had her room in Lowell House.)

What would happen if I changed an entry in a Victim file? First, could I make a permanent change? Second how would the NSA programs - and the Watcher - respond?

I now used four different greynet avatars for my spying. I chose one from Montreal, Canada and hacked in. Selecting an African-American Victim file at random, I deleted the two minus signs in her file. Then I sat back, sipped my coffee, and waited.

Nothing happened.

After two more cups of coffee and a walk in the morning sunshine, nothing had happened.

Could it be that the AO Directorate did not have a program to monitor changes in their own files? This was hard to believe. Yet Stavisky always said bureaucrats were dunces who were dead from the neck up.

Also, the NSA programming was created through government contracting. Was it possible that NSA - or the AO Directorate - did not purchase an internal security program to watch their own files?

I considered the point. If the entire focus was on external hacking, this might be true. The purchasing officer who wrote the NSA procurement scope might assume all threats would be external. Thus the NSA would not pay for an internal program to watch itself.

What would happen if I added a minus or a plus to someone's file? I would not try that now. I did not want to push my luck. Somehow deleting a "minus" from a file seemed different from creating one.

I learned the meaning of the "minuses" sooner than expected.

My mother's blog had grown to a national rallying site. Hadassah AgOp was known throughout the community of American Jews. In addition to reporting their stories, she now published opinion pieces by authors across the anti-TAgOp spectrum.

My mother's notoriety produced one unexpected consequence. Since traditional media, like The New York Times and old-line broadcast networks, would not challenge leftist orthodoxy, Hadassah AgOp now became a regular on the conservative radio talk shows she used to despise. They alone were unafraid of the truth.

Which is how I discovered the meaning of the minuses.

Hadassah AgOp had received her minuses because she had attracted the attention of the wrong people. The minuses then triggered government action.

Soon after the minuses appeared in my mother's file, my parents received an audit notice from the IRS.

My parents had always filed squeaky-clean tax returns. This was my father's compulsion. He did not discuss it much; occasionally, however, he would make a comment that he had backup for every expense and income item in every return my parents ever filed.

The audit notice was not just a simple desk audit. It required my parents to produce every back-up receipt for every item of income or deduction on their last six years' tax returns. This was also a red flag. The usual statute of limitations - the time limit for the IRS to review your returns - is three years. Only if they suspect fraud do they go back six years. So a six-year IRS audit was way, way outside the norm.

When my parents told me, I knew what it was. Three minuses, in their case, meant a savage tax audit.

What other government abuses followed three minuses in a Victim file?

Now that I knew more, I did a random check of individuals who had received three minuses in the Victim files. It was easy; I googled their names to find reports of government abuse.

The pattern was the same; only the type of outrage differed. People with three minuses were subject to tax audits, OSHA audits, EPA enforcement actions, indictments for civil rights violations or sex harassment, and - most common for Republicans, campaign funding violations. The victims suffered not only legal costs, financial destruction, and the possibility of jail – but the intent was clearly to make them pariahs in their communities.

Could the effect of "minuses" be reversed?

What would happen if I deleted the minuses from a Victim file?

It would be hard to learn the result for a person I did not know. In other words, even if I knew from Google that a person was the target of an EPA enforcement, it would be hard to find out how (if at all) things changed after I deleted the minuses.

There were, of course, two people I did know – my parents.

It would be risky for them if I tampered with their file and were discovered. On the other hand, if I successfully covered my tracks, who would know that I tampered with their file?

It was a risk I had to take.

The next day, using a greynet avatar from Missouri, I changed my mother's file. It would be too much, I thought, to change her minuses to pluses. So I simply deleted the minuses.

Then I waited.

My parents were scheduled to bring their papers to the IRS Manhattan office on October 20th. To prepare, they had met with their accountant and filled two suitcases with six years' worth of documents.

Six days after I changed the file they received notice that the October meeting was cancelled. Also, due to a change of circumstances, the notice said, the matter would now be limited to a review (i.e., not an in-person audit) of only the last tax return they had filed. After that review, the IRS would send them a list of questions - if any - still needing answers.

My parents were elated. They thought the government had just recognized its mistake in selecting them for a fraud audit. I, of course, knew the truth.

I had not discussed any of this with Sarah or Stavisky.

Several days later Sarah and I were sitting by the Charles doing a math problem when I had another lightning insight. If I could change the minuses in a Victim file, what else could I change?

I immediately knew the answer; but it would take a while before the full import became clear.

23

The Jewish holidays came early that year.

As in the story of the Rabbi's mice, except for the Shabbos service where I met Sarah and the Seder at Hillel, I had not been to services since my bar mitzvah. Sarah now persuaded me to attend Rosh Hashanah service with her. She had found a tiny "free" Reform congregation in Brookline that was open to anyone who wished to attend.

"Don't worry," she joked. "You'll be able to follow the service. This is for people like you who don't remember what they learned for their bar mitzvah!"

So that Rosh Hashanah morning we found our way to a small two-story building tucked away on a side street in Brookline. Inside was standing room only. It was as if the congregants, of all shapes and sizes, and seemingly from all walks of life, were drawn here to seek their common identity as defense against the public onslaught.

I don't remember much about that service except for the Torah portion. The Rosh Hashanah reading is the story of Abraham and Isaac on Mount Moriah.

God calls to Abraham, and Abraham answers, "Hineni" – "Here am I."

God then tells Abraham to take his son Isaac, "whom you love," to the land of Moriah and offer him there as a burnt offering.

Of course you know the rest of the story. Abraham, trusting in God, takes Isaac to the mountain and prepares to sacrifice him. As Abraham raises the knife, an angel of the Lord calls out to him. "Abraham! Abraham!"

Abraham answers, "Hineni" – "Here am I." The angel then says, "Do not raise your hand against the boy, or do anything to him. For now I know that you fear God, since you have not withheld your son, you only son, from Me."

The Lord provides a ram for a substitute sacrifice in place of the boy, and the angel of the Lord then calls out a second time:

"By myself, I swear, the Lord declares: Because you have done this and not withheld your son, your only son, I will bestow my blessing upon you and make your descendants as numerous as the stars of heaven and the sands on the seashore…All the nations of the earth shall bless themselves by your descendants, because you have obeyed my command."**

   The rest of that day I kept thinking about the Torah portion. Through the millennia since that event the nations of the earth had indeed been blessed by so many gifts of Jewish genius - but they had not blessed themselves by us.

   We were an infinitesimal percentage of humanity. Unlike other religions we did not proselytize or seek domination. All we wanted was to be left alone. Yet in every generation they came for us.

   "Hineni," I thought. Why did that one phrase resonate so much with me?

** Genesis, 22. Modified translation based on Tanakh, Jewish Publication Society (1999 ed.).

24

Meanwhile the teeth of Part Two began to bite. There were now hundred of stories of Jews losing their jobs or being denied admission to colleges and professional schools. We also began to hear more and more stories of Jews packing up and leaving.

Hadassah AgOp now had fifteen or twenty such reports every day. At first she was hesitant to publish them. She was not sure whether it was right.

My mother told us these stories were the tip of the iceberg. If you had decided to leave the country - and you needed to liquidate your possessions - you would keep it quiet; and the more prominent you were, the quieter you would want to be.

The United States was now, also, in its worst recession of the 21st Century. From reports in the media, from the experiences of people we knew, and from stories sent to Hadassah AgOp, "recession" was a euphemism.

The cumulative result of what people now called "Obamanomics", plus the stifling effect of the Victims Law, was a dead economy - and this was before Part Two began to excise Jews from the marketplace. The only financial life force came from the accelerating high-tech revolution, which continued to transform our lives while it cut the need for paid labor.

American Jews now faced the same terrible question their ancestors faced in pre-war Nazi Germany, in Czarist Russia, in 12th Century England, in Moorish Spain[††], and in how many other places – to go or not to go?

In every age it was always that one question.

Is it better, for your family's survival, to pack up and leave everything? Or is it better to gamble that this will pass? Is this just a matter of the ruling party's temporary political expediency? Will things of course change when people come to their senses?

Just to state such questions made them clichés. Yet each family must reach its own decision, with different impacts on different families.

We were all Americans. Many had deep roots in communities where we had raised our children, made friends, become part of the social web. To uproot ourselves - think of uprooting a large tree - would be utterly destructive. It would mean great, if not complete,

---

†† And then later the Spain of the Inquisition.

financial loss. It would break up families. It would cause who knew what other tragedy.

These issues were almost more difficult for secular Jews to whom religious observance had no meaning. Many no longer even self-identified as Jews. If asked, they would say they had no religion. They were just Americans. They had no part in archaic observances that did not comport with their modern identity.

Why should they be punished for the sins of long-forgotten ancestors? Why should they be treated like the black-hat Orthodox, whom they viewed as strange if not completely alien? It was not just unfair but outrageous!

25

In a surprise to both of us, Sarah's parents were the first we knew who decided to go.

Sarah was shocked. It was one thing to read stories in the media. It was another to get a call from your parents saying they were picking up and leaving the United States.

Sarah's father was a senior executive at a large aerospace firm. Her mother was a tax lawyer, a partner in a small but highly regarded New York firm.

"It wasn't my Jewish mother!" Sarah told me. "It was my Mandarin dad! Mom was on-the-one-hand, on-the-other hand. A typical lawyer! But Dad remembers the Cultural Revolution in China. He knows what happens when a government picks a class of enemies. He says now is the time. He won't wait until they close the borders! And he says they will close the borders!"

This news scared us badly. It was not just that Sarah's family would be riven. (She had to decide if she would go, too - which put me in the mix.) It was that life as we knew it - our American life - was crumbling around us.

The news compelled Sarah to tell her parents about me. "I have to tell them," she said, "because they have to know why I can't go with them. I can't imagine a life without you."

Sarah's parents were not surprised. In fact, they had expected something like this. They said they knew from many signs that something was different in her life. "Many signs of Sunlight," said her father.

They were very happy for her. They asked, of course, to meet me, the person now responsible for the indefinite severance of their small family.

So the next Friday we took the train to New York.

Sarah's parents lived in a small brownstone in the West Village, which they had scraped to buy many years ago. Now it was in the middle of ultra chic.

I didn't know what to expect. Of course I was nervous - like any suitor meeting the parents of his intended. But the reality could not have been easier. It was as if I had always been a member of the Po family.

Sarah's mother was more or less what I expected - a trim, well-dressed New York Jewish woman, light brown hair, horn-rimmed glasses, quick tongue. You might have met her at a UJA planning session or a charity benefit, or a school meeting.

Her father was not what I expected (although I was not sure what I had expected). Tall and distinguished, he wore the dark pinstriped suit of a lawyer or banker. He combined Asian tranquility with the imposing demeanor of a senior executive.

You would not have thought of either as flight refugees, about to drop all and flee America.

"Sarah has told us about you," said Charles Po. He smiled. "Of course we can't tell you what she said! But it was good."

"A nice Jewish boy who just happens to be a math genius!" quipped Ruth Po, less constrained by confidentiality.

They had known something was up with Sarah, they repeated for my benefit, because she seemed always happy now - definitely much less moody than before Harvard.

They asked me questions about myself, to get me talking - which I did for a while. Then, somberly, they turned to their departure.

"It is our Exodus," said Mr. Po. "And others are now leaving, too. You can read it in the newspapers - not just in your mother's blog. (Sarah had told them about Hadassah AgOp.) This is the beginning of the "ExUs", the Exodus from the United States. We are the early ones. We are leaving before Moses arrives; but there will surely come a Moses."

They told us about plans they had made to liquidate investments and transfer cash out of the country. They had been doing it in increments so as not to draw attention.

Mr. Po said they were going first to Canada. They would simply drive across the border like tourists. They had rented a condo in Montreal.

At the outset they wanted to stay close to the U.S. so they could watch what happened - and be near Sarah if she chose not to leave with them but later changed her mind. Then, from Montreal, they would decide what to do next.

Mr. Po said they would have enough to live decently if not luxuriously. He said they had set up bank accounts in several countries, which they could access as needed. Perhaps most important, when the TAG Op Regs were first published, anticipating the worst, they had bought a condo in a country which granted 'economic' residence visas. If they could not stay in

Canada or find another country they preferred, they had their port in the storm.‡‡

Mrs. Po began to cry as he finished speaking. "I can't believe this is happening," she said.

"Of course it is happening," said Mr. Po. "The Jews of America have forgotten their Haggadah. In every generation they come. And we Chinese know, also, that there is always change. Bad times always alternate with good ones."

They had decided, they said, that there was no point in delaying further. They would leave the following week.

They hugged each of us as we left.

"Take care of the Six Green Harmony," Mr. Po said to Sarah. He reached out and touched the necklace, then gently touched her face. Sarah was clearly the light of their lives.

---

‡‡ Because of the sudden outflow of American Jews, most nations offering 'economic' citizenship or residence soon sold out their existing allotment of such visas. Some such countries then decided to stop their visa offerings. Others, however, sensing a huge opportunity, vastly increased their available visas. Also, a number of countries that previously had no such programs now decided to create them to catch the financial tide of the Jews fleeing America.

My beautiful Sarah and I took the long train ride back to Boston. We looked out the window and watched the passing coastline. It was a quiet trip.

The next week Charles and Ruth Po left their American life and drove into Canada.

26

Two days later the President issued a new Executive Order to slow the outflow of Jews.

The media speculated that this happened because of White House panic.

With daily reports of emigrating Jews, said the pundits, the Administration must be afraid of a serious economic downturn. There must also be worry about bad press throughout the world.

As if, Ari said, the White House would not have considered such things when they engineered the whole AgOp thing!

The new Executive Order required any AgOp leaving the country to file a 30-day "Exit Notice" with the Bureau of Immigration and Customs Enforcement (ICE).

The Exit Notice was complex. It required the departing AgOp to report his or her itinerary outside the U.S. and return date. It also required a list of all assets which the AgOp owned - and all his or her asset sales, as well as asset sales of any parents or children, within the last six months.

After receiving the Exit Notice, ICE would advise within 30 days whether the particular Jew could leave the country. More than half such requests were denied on grounds of alleged defects in the Exit Notice. A re-filing was then required, which started the process from the beginning.

After getting the Exit Notices, of course, ICE knew which Jews wanted to leave and what property they owned.

American Jews now became more desperate.

While they could not sell their homes or other real estate overnight, they could sell stocks and bonds - and proceeded to do so. Consequently, the day after the President issued the Exit Notice Executive Order, the stock and bond markets crashed, with panic selling unlike anything since 1929. Each day thereafter the markets dropped incrementally further.

The American economy ground to a halt. Businesses froze expansion plans. Conventions and business meetings were cancelled (and those events which did proceed were funereal).

No one knew what to do.

Non-Jews had two responses to the collapsing markets.

Those who favored the TAgOp Regs (meaning many beneficiaries of the Victims Law, many non-Jewish liberal Democrats, university faculties, and U.S. Muslims) blamed the Jews for the new financial crisis.

This was, they said, just another example of Jewish economic manipulation in a long history of such manipulations. They called for sanctions and penalties against any Jew selling assets. MAFR went further, calling for the President to close the borders completely.

Most other Americans decried the Exit Notices. There were, in fact, huge public protests by concerned citizens who saw their country being destroyed. But they had no power; and the Administration ignored them.

In response to public concern and to allow a return to more orderly markets (or so the White House press release stated), the President ordered the SEC to suspend trading on all exchanges for one week.

One conservative journalist reported that the President even considered martial law but was talked out of this by aides. When asked about this at the press briefing on the market suspension, however, the White House Press Secretary derided the very idea.

Jews now were frantic. Thousands filed the Exit Notice, hoping to depart. Seats sold out on airlines, cruise ships, and trains. There was a rush for the exits for all who hoped to get ICE approval.

The country was now in the worst economic downturn since 2008-2009. Asset prices of all types plummeted. Speculators bought Jewish homes and other properties at fractional values.

The end of the Exit Notice turmoil was perhaps predictable.

Just two months after the Executive Order requiring the Exit Notice, the President issued another Executive Order closing the borders. It was, said the President, for the preservation of order and domestic tranquility.

There would be no further AgOp departures.

Ari said the President was the new Pharaoh. "Now we must go to the President and say, "Let our people go!" he said. But he did not laugh when he said it.

Given the advanced DNA technology used to administer the Victims Law, the border closing was easy to enforce.

Each person leaving the country had to submit to a digital DNA swipe by an ICE officer. Within seconds the computer showed your Victim status. If you were a Jew trying to escape, you were immediately arrested for felony emigration violation. Your property was forfeit; and you went to jail.

27

After these events my parents were terrified. Despite my father's cautious investing, the collapsing market had reduced his portfolio from $4 million to $800,000.

My mother was working 18-hour days.

Hadassah AgOp was deluged with stories of financial ruin and destroyed families, of Jews wondering what would happen to them. They sought her advice as if she - unbearably distressed herself - had some magic or divine anodyne.

In turn, every other night now my parents called me - as if I, too, might have some magical answer. Of course I did not.

(We knew, of course, that the government listened to all our calls; so, even though we were careful in what we said, we almost didn't care. It would not make any difference.)

"We should have left when we had the chance, like the Pos" said my father.

I had told them about Sarah's parents. While they found it hard to believe that someone could be

Jewish and Chinese, the rule was clear. Sarah had a Jewish mother, so she was Jewish. They said they could not wait to meet her.

On each call my father bemoaned their market losses. "And what next?" he asked. "Our City pensions. They'll cut off our pensions for sure!"

"They can't do that!" said my mother. "But who knows? They'll find a pretext! Why don't they let us go if they hate us so much?"

"They can't let us go," said my father. "What would it say to the world, to their own ideology, if they opened the door and we all ran out? Besides, they want to keep our money."

"If they let us go, they could blame us for the whole collapse!" said my mother. "For the disintegration of American society - because that is what is happening."

"Would you leave if you could?" I asked.

"If that were legally possible, yes," said my father. It was as if he were speaking to the government listeners.

"Of course," said my mother. "But it isn't! Not legally possible. How could we do what is not possible?"

And so it went, every other night.

Sarah heard from her parents at least once a week. Occasionally they spoke by phone. But, her father being very cautious, they communicated mainly by coded emails. (Before they left Sarah had worked out a simple code with her father. The communications back and forth seemed plain vanilla; but within the simple clichéd sentences were real messages.)

Charles and Ruth were still in Montreal but were considering a move to Vancouver, a possible jumping off place to the country in which they had their condo residence visa. They had of course wanted Sarah to join them; but this now seemed impossible.

Montreal was flooded with American Jews who had made it out before the border closing, as were Toronto and other parts of Canada.

To their great credit, most Canadians welcomed the Jews and decried the actions of the American government. The Prime Minister introduced legislation to grant special temporary resident status to incoming American Jews. If it passed, Charles and Ruth could stay in Canada indefinitely.

With the border closing, Sarah seemed doomed to be separated from her parents for who knew how long - if not forever. And my own parents faced a permanent grim future in New York City (although I really did not know if they would flee if they could).

Ari's parents, too, were stuck. His father, a senior neurosurgeon at Weill Cornell New York Hospital, had lost his position two months before the border closings. He received the same type of "legal compliance notice" as had my parents.

Ari's mother was a traditional mom who had stayed home to take care of Ari and his older sister, a curator at the Metropolitan Museum. They were comfortable, if not hugely wealthy.

Coincidentally, like Sarah's parents, they owned a vacation condo in a Caribbean country that gave them economic citizenship if they could ever get there.

Unlike Sarah's parents, who had bought their condo specifically in response to the TAgOp Regs, the Cohens had bought their condo on a lark ten years before. When they bought the condo they took the citizenship as a joke, never thinking it might be a life raft. Now, of course, they could not get to their 'adoptive' country.

In such dark days, Ari did not joke as much (although he still could not resist an occasional shot).

He had become very interested in writings of Jewish sages who had experienced the recurrent uprooting and massacres of our history.

"You know," he told me, "it's amazing that any of us have survived at all. Statistically it's almost impossible. Most people know about the Holocaust. They know about 1492 and the expulsion from Spain. Maybe they know about Russian pogroms. But this has happened everywhere! In every century! In almost every county where we have lived!"

"But not in America and not in the American centuries," I said.

"No. Not in the American centuries," Ari said. "Until now. But now it is happening here!"

"So what can we do?" I asked.

Ari shook his head. He had no answer.

And, with no answer to that question, life went on in Cambridge.

Sarah attended classes, and I dug deeper into the NSA files.

The one change now was in the ever-present anti-Semitism. It was sometimes subtle, sometimes overt, but lurking in so many daily encounters.

The BDS student groups were more and more aggressive. Anti-Israel BDS t-shirts, and also black-and-white Palestinian keffiyehs, were all over the campus.

My old nemesis, Mahmoud, had a weekly rally - on Saturday, the Jewish Sabbath - calling for the expulsion of all Jews from Harvard.

Jewish students travelled in groups to avoid being beaten on the street.

We began to hear rumors of Jews sneaking across to Canada in off-road wilderness areas away from the Customs crossing points. This was highly risky, of course. If you were caught, you got an automatic, ten-year jail sentence without parole.

Then, after the media started to report on the escapes through the wilderness, ICE suddenly became highly effective at catching Jews. ICE announced a 95% catch rate, which was amazing in contrast to its prior record of failing to catch illegal Mexicans!

28

It was while Sarah and I were doing an afternoon math problem by the Charles that I had the "un-Mohel"[§§] idea.

"Wouldn't it be wonderful if we could just go?" said Sarah. "Just cross the border. Just leave all this craziness. Your parents could go. Ari's parents could go. We could see my parents. We could find a place to start new lives."

She touched the Six Green Harmony as if for strength.

And there was the idea, so obvious in its simplicity.

I said nothing to Sarah. The next morning, however, when she left for class, I dug into the NSA files.

[§§] A "mohel" is the person who performs the rite of circumcision on male Jews at the age of eight days. Circumcision is the mark of God's covenant with Abraham: "This shall be my covenant in your flesh, an eternal covenant." In my case, to be the "un-Mohel" would be digitally to reverse the sign of the covenant, to convert a Jew back into a non-Jew.

The idea was this - if I could alter the pluses and minuses, why could I not change a person's DNA record?

Why could I not make a Jew a gentile? And, if so, would the Watcher see what I had done?

I picked a random TAgOp file - Jeremy Goldstein, a common Jewish name. I looked at the coding behind the file. It was really simple.

As I guessed before and had discussed with Stavisky, the NSA code-writers did not consider, apparently, that the NSA files could be hacked from within. Or they did not want to spend government money on more internal security.

What would happen to a Jew if I made him or her a non-Jew?

Of course I would also need to confer a new Victim status, so that everything was seamless. But what would happen? Other than that he or she could fit into the ordinary Victim status, which would otherwise accrue to them as a white man or woman.

Would my new gentile be caught at the border?

Or could he or she simply stroll across to freedom?

How could I test this out? It would take great care. It would be wrong and dangerous to try such a change on anyone who did not know.

I considered the ramifications. To be suddenly changed from Jew to non-Jew, the "changee" would be caught by complete surprise. He or she would not know what to do. In a panic the changee might give away the whole show - let alone likely going to jail and losing all because I had messed with his or her DNA file.

I took the "T" to North Boston and went for a long walk on the waterfront as I had done in the past when trying to solve a really knotty problem. Walking the piers always seemed to unravel knots in the mind.

Halfway through my walk I had the answer. I would be my own guinea pig.

It was obvious. How could I even think of trying this on anyone else? I must change my own file and attempt the border crossing myself.

That night I decided to tell Sarah. It was a tough choice.

As long as Sarah knew nothing, she was safe. However, once Sarah knew what I had been doing - and intended to do - she would be at risk for the rest of her life.

How could I do that to her?

Yet what I planned - success or failure - would directly impact Sarah's future with me. And even if she knew nothing, federal enforcers would never believe her. How could she, my love and lover, with her own record of computer hacking, know nothing?

So I told her.

She was not surprised. She knew me so well that she had known I was up to something.

"You have to take me with you!" she said. "It's very simple. You can't do this alone!"

Her response was immediate, with no hint of doubt.

It was far, far too risky, I said. "Just by telling you I have put you in danger. How could I forgive myself - ever - if you went to jail, or worse, because they caught me at the border? It's beyond reckless!"

"But it's not reckless," Sarah said.

"You clearly have this figured out," she continued. "Remember, of all people, I know how smart you really are. And I'm a hacker, too! There has never been anyone quite like you! I know!"

We argued back and forth for more than an hour; then, beyond argument but without resolution, we went to bed and made slow love.

In the end we decided that Sarah would not attempt that first crossing with me. Instead she would drive with me to the Canadian border and wait for my return.

29

I now had to plan the real event.

The mechanics were easy. I would just convert my V-status into 100% male Caucasian.

Even though I was an expert on the government file structures, I was still suspicious of the apparent simplicity of the Victim files. There had to be more, I thought, than just the status coding for different types of ancestry.

There were, indeed, numerical status codes for different types of ethnic ancestry. I had found these by following the technical map of the NSA programming.

When your DNA was swiped, the computers compared your DNA matrix to DNA models in the files; after finding the right match, they inserted the corresponding numerical combination into your V-file - which then showed on your V-Cert as Caucasian, Chinese, African, Mongol, etc. Or Ashkenazi Jew.

It was not complex programming, however, and after numerous probes I had found nothing more. (That Jews were treated separately from Caucasians or other racial ethnic groups, of course, showed thoughtful advance planning by someone.)

I studied random white male V-files to see if there were other markers I should take into account. I found none.

Was this simplicity just the result of one-dimensional stupidity in the NSA's procurement of the contract for the programming? Or was it somehow intentional?

This led me to hunt for the identity of the government programmers. I should have thought of this before. Better late than never, however, to get to know your enemy.

With very little digging, I learned the NSA had awarded the software contract to a firm that specialized in creating purchasing programs for federal and state procurement agencies. The firm's programs helped the agencies buy goods and services and hire construction contractors. The firm also helped merchants create identity web sites with shopping cart functions.

How did expertise in creating purchasing and shopping cart websites qualify my enemy to write NSA programs of great complexity? The answer was not obvious on its face.

Yet this same firm had received a "sole source" contract for the NSA work. This meant someone high up in the Administration thought their expertise so special that it brooked no competition.

Or perhaps, as I quickly learned, there was more.

The firm's real secret - the key to "sole source" status - was their CEO's college friendship with the Attorney General. Add to which that this same CEO had been a leading bundler of contributions for every one of the President's political campaigns. What better credentials to justify "sole source"?

Of course, such a "special" relationship might mean that the CEO's firm was one of few whom the government could trust with advance knowledge of its plans to crush the Jews.

It was the perfect wedding of crony capitalism and national security.

Given this new knowledge, and knowing the simple structure of the NSA coding, I guessed that the enemy did not have many Einsteins on their payroll.

The new knowledge did not change my plans. But it gave me a perspective on why the NSA files were so poorly planned.

I had to assume, however, that if the government had no Einstein now, they would find one quickly if they discovered what I was doing.

There were still many variables.

If I just changed my DNA file to non-Jew, what about my ancestors?

I had to dig further into the files than I had before.

The V-Cert, or non-Cert, or AgOp Cert - only showed percentage of ancestry - it did not show the history of your ancestors. Was all your ancestral information in the DNA, or did the files have detailed history on your ancestors?[***] How much detail was behind those percentages in the NSA file?

For several days I tried to trace DNA chains to actual ancestors. It was a dead end.

There were, of course, several commercial websites that let you trace your ancestry quite far back. It would have been expensive, however, and fraught with problems, for NSA programmers to try to correlate such actual ancestry chains with the DNA programming.

Also, since the DNA models gave the government what they really needed - verified blood ancestry by percentage - they could skip the actual histories (which might not in fact be accurate).

[***] Except for whatever information you had self-certified in your pre-pin prick filing under the Victims Law.

Would there be a daisy-chain effect if I changed only my own file? In other words, had the programmers written an algorithm to ring an alarm if the last link in my DNA chain were changed to be inconsistent with my prior ancestral characterization?

This was different from just changing pluses and minuses.

I picked a random white male and studied the code behind his V-file. I soon realized that it was passive. While the DNA swipe revealed your blood ancestry, the program simply recorded the applicable number code for the DNA model. It was not inter-active. It did not review prior history.

So no alarm should go off if I changed the end result from Ashkenazi Jew to male Caucasian.

The next question was how long it would need for a change to take effect throughout the government systems. The timing would be critical.

If I made the change too far in advance, it would allow more time for the Watcher to catch me. If I did it too close to the event, there might be a delay in file processing (the government systems were not lightning fast) so that I would be caught at the border.

Also, I would need a new non-V Cert. I decided on a one-week window – I would make the change one week before I attempted the crossing.

30

And now it was time. One sunny morning I went into my NSA file and changed the final code entry to 100 % Caucasian male. I then had the system send my new non-V-Cert to an email address in Idaho (which I was able to print out when received).

Seven days later Sarah and I rented a car and drove to Burlington, Vermont. There we took a room in a chain motel where she would wait for my return.

It was now late October. It had been a cold, rainy autumn; most of the leaves were gone.

We had dinner in a funky local Burlington restaurant. They did not ask for our V-Certs. Life seemed so normal. Vermont was what we thought small-town life should be. You would not have known America was collapsing around us.

The next day, wearing a blue blazer and jeans (to look as preppy as possible), with my passport and new V-Cert in hand, I drove to the border near Stanstead, Quebec.

On the U.S. side a new facility had been recently constructed to require U.S. screening in the outbound lane. (Previously outbound cars just went to Canadian customs; only inbound cars had been required to pass through U.S. Customs.)

There was a line of about fifteen cars ahead of me. Because ICE had to do the DNA swipe on everyone, the border crossing now took much longer.

Standing at the station were two ICE agents with the little DNA swipers, one for each side of the car.

The process was simple, like the swipe of your ticket when you board an airplane. You held out your hand to the agent. The agent swiped the swiper against your skin. There was a delay of 30 seconds. If a green light flashed, they waved you through. If a red light flashed, they did not wave you through - and you went to jail.

It was the longest 30 seconds of my life.

Finally a green light flashed, and they waved me through.

I stepped on the accelerator. I was in Canada – and I was no longer a Jew.

I pulled the car over at nearest rest area and got out. It was raining a slow drizzle. I was exhausted, as if I had just run a long distance. I had done it; but what had I done? What had I begun?

I sent an email to Sarah - "Parcel delivered." Then I found another chain motel on the outskirts of Sherbrooke to stay the night.

We had decided it would look better if I stayed overnight than if I just turned around and crossed back immediately. If questioned as to the purpose of my visit, I would say I was applying for a summer fellowship at McGill and seeking an interview. But no one asked.

The return was uneventful. There was such great focus on stopping Jewish escapees that ICE almost didn't care who entered the U.S. They certainly would not expect any escaped Jew to return!

We stayed another night in the Burlington motel, and then drove back to Cambridge.

We had, of course, many questions. How long would it be before the NSA discovered my switch? I had to assume they would not sleep forever.

Should I go back and re-switch my identity - make myself Jewish once again? Or might that attract even more attention?

We decided that I would stay what I was.

This meant that if I was going to help other Jews leave, there was probably a timed window before I - and they - would be discovered. So we had to act quickly.

And that was my new task, of course - to help other Jews leave. That is what I had now begun.

31

We decided to start with my parents. I called and told them I was coming for a quick visit and bringing a friend.

Sarah and I had decided to take the train to New York. We got only as far as Back Bay Station.

Standing in front of the ticket booth was an ICE agent. He was doing a DNA swipe of every ticket buyer.

When we approached, I went first and got the same green light as at the Canadian border. Sarah got a red light. "Sorry," said the agent. "You can't buy a ticket. No AgOps allowed on this train."

Stunned, we turned and left the ticket line.

Returning to Cambridge, we arranged to borrow Ari's car and then drove to New York.

My parents had a triple shock.

The first shock was Sarah. I had never brought a girl home to meet them. And Sarah looked beautifully Chinese even if I told them she was a nice Jewish girl!

The second was that Sarah and I had been together for a long time in what was clearly a very serious relationship.

And the third, of course, which really blew them away, was my proposal that they leave the country.

"How can we just pick up and leave?" asked my mother. She kept staring at Sarah as if the evidence of her eyes would not let her believe that Sarah was Jewish.

"Of course we can - and we have to!" said my father. "It's clear as a bell. And there will be no other chance! You know we have been discussing this. We have even transferred money to Canada."

[It was still possible to transfer funds in increments of less than $10,000 per day without filing a report, although everyone knew that would soon end.] "We've been thinking about this for a long time."

"Thinking is not doing," said my mother. "Thinking is not doing."

This debate actually lasted only a few minutes.

My mother and father kept looking back and forth at each other and then at Sarah and me. They knew there was no choice. They had to go. It was now or never.

We explained the procedure. They would do exactly what Sarah and I had done - drive to Vermont, stay overnight, and then cross the border.

They would go the following week, and I would make the change in their NSA files tomorrow.

"How did you do this? How did you figure this out?" my father asked.

"I can't tell you," I said. "Frankly, we shouldn't even have told you that I am the one."

I looked at Sarah. "We need to think how we tell people that this is arranged."

Sarah looked at me and reflexively touched the Six Green Harmony. "Maybe in the future we should tell people that we know a person who does this," she said. "Yes. We'll say we know someone important who is asking us to act as intermediary. Then the word will spread as we help more people."

I agreed. "For their safety and for ours, I can't be the one to deal directly with anyone," I said.

"Who thought that teaching you algebra at six would lead to this," said my father with a sigh. He was both proud and perplexed. "Mini-Einstein becomes Mini-Moses!"

"Hardly," I said. "Just a computer geek who has figured a way to help out."

Thus the next day I changed my parents into gentiles; and one week later they crossed successfully into Canada.

We had told them, of course, how to contact Sarah's parents; so they all met in Montreal.

By the reports of both mothers, it was a great meeting. They certainly had a lot to discuss. Sarah's mother wrote that they talked for five hours straight.

Sarah's parents helped mine to find a small condo rental where they could live while they figured out what to do next. Unlike Sarah's parents, however, my father and mother did not have the hidey-hole of economic citizenship in another country. They had to plan what would happen if and when Canada came looking for them. (Canada had still not passed the refuge law for American Jews proposed by the Prime Minister.)

Since she wrote in cyberspace, my mother did not have to leave behind the Hadassah AgOp blog. I was able to set her up with an offshore web link that made it seem as if Hadassah still originated from New York.

Hadassah AgOp thus continued to report to the world on the gripping tragedies of American Jews.

32

Sarah and I now faced a dilemma. What to do next? Should we leave while we could, before I was discovered? Or, should we commit ourselves to helping as many Jews as possible to get out?

Could I do the same thing from outside the country? There were no borders on cyber-hacking.

Or should I stay in the U.S., because I could be more effective here in person. But, if I stayed, should Sarah go?

"These are not choices," she said. "Of course you must do this! Of course you must stay here! And of course I must stay. I will not leave you here alone. Besides, you can't do this without me. I am your intermediary. I am the one who will tell people that an important person is asking me to do this. You will be in the background."

She was determined, and she was right. We had to speak to prospective departees (we had started to call them "departees") in person, not by phone or email. For now Sarah would be the person who started that conversation.

"Also", Sarah said, "We have to assume, from now on, that every little thing we do is watched."

186

There was also the question of how much we should try to do. Would it be selfish just to help people we knew?

Or did we have a duty to help as many as possible? The answer to such a question was, unfortunately, clear from the outset. We had to try to help as many as possible.

I was a computer geek and mathematician, never interested in politics or social issues. Now I faced great issues of right and wrong, at great personal risk to Sarah and myself - possibly even life or death, if not long incarceration.

What we were planning was highly illegal if not treasonous to our country, far more serious in scale than just sneaking one or two Jews across the border.

Awed by these prospects, we decided to start small, just with people we knew and cared about. Also, since I was no logistics expert, we knew our first efforts would be hit or miss; but we had to start somewhere.

That somewhere would be Ari.

We met him for coffee at Starbucks.

"Einstein and the Chinese Maideleh!" he joked. "To what do I owe this extraordinary honor?"

We explained that we knew someone who could help him and his family to leave the U.S.

He became instantly serious. "And who is this someone and how can this someone do this?" he asked.

We said we could not, for obvious reasons, tell him who it was. I explained, however, that this someone had the ability to change the federal computer files on a person's identity - from Jew to not-Jew - so that when you crossed the border, the DNA swipe would let you through.

"An un-Mohel!" Ari joked. "This "someone" is a person who can reverse the work of the Mohel!"

He paused, then laughed. "And what would happen if the border police make you drop trou for inspection? That would be a different type of DNA test, no?"

"That wouldn't matter," I said. "Look, these days many non-Jews are circumcised - and remember, all Muslims are circumcised, too!"

"And who could this person be who is smart enough to figure this all out - AND get into the federal computer files?" Ari said, looking at me. "Do we know anyone that smart? Who could that possibly, possibly be?"

"The identity is a secret," Sarah said. "We don't know; but we just know someone who does."

"Of course you don't know," said Ari. "Sure. And if you expect me to believe that, you have a bridge for sale from my hometown to Manhattan. But, not to worry, I will never say who this secret genius might be." He put his right hand over his eyes. "I have already forgotten what I of course never knew in the first place!"

Then he became serious.

"You are asking a lot," he said. 'My parents and I are just supposed to take your word for it? Gamble our freedom and future? Suppose it's a trap, a set-up? You are asking a lot."

"It isn't a trap," I said. "It's for real. We know it works." Then I told him the story how I myself had crossed into Canada and returned, and that then we had sent my parents across.

That got his attention.

"I believe you," he said. "I believe you because I know this someone is really you - or else you would not even propose this to me. You don't have to say anything. Needless to say, I will discuss this with my parents. I think we will all say yes. What other answer is there?"

He stopped and grimaced at me. "But if you plan to approach other people, you need to create a better story."

Sarah and I were silent. Our silence was concurrence.

So ten days later, Ari, his parents, and his sister went to JFK for a flight to the Caribbean. Their DNA swipes flashed green, and they were gone to a new life.

33

What to do next?

We had to find a safe way to contact as many Jews as possible who might wish to leave. Since we could not advertise on TV, or radio, or on the web, and since we could not just approach Jews on the street, it was a dilemma.

We decided that I would discuss the problem with Professor Stavisky, in part because Sarah and I had decided he would be our next departee.

Although he and I had talked about keeping up regular meetings, I had seen him less and less since the end of the NSA gig, for obvious reasons.

So Stavisky was surprised when I appeared in his office one afternoon with a crazy proposition.

"I needed something to brighten my day," he said. "I was just sitting here staring blankly at a screen of code - and throwing darts at my Jew Cert!"

He said he expected Harvard to evict him from this office by the end of the semester. They knew he had lost the NSA assignment; but they only acted on a semester-by-semester basis.

"I have a crazy proposition for you," I said.

He chewed on his pipe stem, waiting.

"How would you like to leave the country?" I asked.

Stavisky sat straight up and peered intently at me. "What are you saying?" he asked.

I told him that I knew someone who could change his AgOp file to make him a non-Jew, what we were calling a "departee". He could then simply drive across the border.

"That someone could only be you, of course," he said. "No one else would have the brains or guts - or audacity - to do that!"

More chewing on the pipe stem. "I still think about that day when you answered that stupid test in eight minutes! Of course it is you! Who else but you would have the preposterous idea that you could change me from Jew to not-Jew?"

"Do you want to leave?" I repeated.

He thought for the briefest of moments. "Why not?" he said. "What do I have here? Nothing from nothing!"

He thought for another moment, then shook his head sadly.

"Wrong! Leaving is the wrong answer! I have a better idea!"

He chewed intently on his pipe stem and stared at me.

"For a long time I have had, in fact, "nothing from nothing", he said. "My wife divorced me years ago. My one daughter lives in L.A. and never calls me. For too many years now I wallow in self-pity. I pretend to play war inside the NSA files but with no compass point."

He again shook his head sadly. "Now you come along. You figure all this out. You have the insane idea that you can get Jews out of the country!"

He shook his pipe stem at me. "And of course you need help! Of course you need help! You don't even know how much you need help! And me - what better do I have but to help you? Why not? It will give me something to feel good about! Now I can have something from something - not nothing from nothing!"

I was caught off guard. It was a response I would never have considered.

"How can you help me?" I asked.

"How can I <u>not</u> help you?" Stavisky laughed.

"You can't do this alone," he said. "First, it would be a disaster if you try direct contact with your departees. I like your word, by the way - "departees". A good word. If you try direct contact, there is a huge probability you will get caught - and quickly! Secrets like this don't keep - and never among expanding numbers of people!"

"Second," he continued, "how will you make contact? Walk down the street and ask every Yid if he wants to leave? Not a good idea."

He resumed chewing on the pipe stem. "<u>I</u> can be your interface," he said. "I can help you plan the logistics. For example, don't you think ICE agents will wonder when dozens of Goldsteins and Levines arrive at the border and get green lights on their DNA tests?"

He laughed. "And what about black hats? Do you think for one minute ICE will let even one family of black hats board a plane, even if their DNA lights all flash green?"

I knew immediately that Stavisky was right.

It was perverse, almost wrong. The Jews we could help the easiest would be the most assimilated, those who were outwardly <u>least</u> Jewish. The risk to each

194

departee - and to us -would increase directly in proportion to his or her indicia of Jewish identity.

Stavisky saw that his logic had upset me.

"So what?" he said. "Maybe in the future you can figure out how to help the Goldsteins and the black hats. For now, it is enough that you help some Jews, even if assimilated. It is enough. Dayenu."

"Dayenu" is the refrain in the Haggadah that we recite at Passover. Each of God's miracles of the Exodus would have been enough in itself - "Dayenu" - for the Jewish people to marvel at God's greatness - let alone all the miracles of the Exodus. So, after reciting each successive miracle, we say, "Dayenu".

Dayenu. It would have to be Dayenu. We would help as many as we could - and it would have to be Dayenu.

"So where do we begin?" I asked. "How do you - my new Cossack-Yid project manager - contact large numbers of assimilated Jews?"

"Where do you go to find Jews?" said Stavisky.

"A deli on Sunday morning." I could not resist a joke. As I said it, I missed Ari.

"Try again," said Stavisky.

195

"A shul," I said.

"Of course," said Stavisky. "Or a temple, especially if you are looking for Reform Jews -who will be the most assimilated."

"We must find Jews in Conservative and Orthodox congregations who can get through," I said. "If they are not wearing kippahs or named Cohen, they should have a chance, too."

As I said that, I realized the risk I had created, unthinkingly, for Ari and his parents. But the ICE agents had looked only at the green DNA lights.

"O.K.", said Stavisky. "So we look for them in every temple and shul." More pipe chewing. "The first thing we need, though, is a test congregation. We find a test congregation and I must go to meet with the rabbi."

After further thoughts along this line, we decided that Stavisky should pick a reform congregation in a small New Hampshire city. It was outside the Boston metropolitan area but a short enough drive. He could easily drive out, meet the rabbi, and drive back in one day.

Before Stavisky contacted the New Hampshire rabbi, however, he and I developed the protocol we would follow for the next few months.

Stavisky would phone the rabbi and say he was new in town and looking to join a congregation. Could he meet with the rabbi? No rabbi could refuse such a meeting. At the meeting Stavisky would explain his true purpose and ask if the rabbi would help in finding a family who wished to leave the U.S.

34

That first rabbi, in New Hampshire, was Rickard
Elmman, a tall, graying man in his sixties. He had a
slight limp from an old injury and walked with a cane.

When they met in his office and Stavisky
revealed the true purpose of his visit, Rabbi Elmman was
suspicious, indeed outraged - to the point where he
almost asked Stavisky to leave.

His was a Reform congregation of liberal Jews
who abhorred Republicans and anything they perceived
as sourced on the right.

"Is this some kind of Republican idea?" asked
Rabbi Elmman. Redfaced, he stood up behind his desk,
as if asserting his authority.

"Do your members think Republicans have done
this to them, this TAgOp business?" Stavisky asked
quietly.

Rabbi Elmman had no answer. He was an honest
man, however. He told Stavisky his congregants were in
shock and denial. They felt there must be some colossal
mistake. How could they be treated as Agents of
Oppression - they who had espoused every Progressive

cause? How could a Democratic President have done this to them?

Saying nothing, Stavisky let the silence speak for itself.

"And you are asking them to pick up and leave everything," said Rabbi Elmman.

"We are not asking them to do anything," said Stavisky, chewing the pipe-stem. "We are offering them escape. We are offering them a new life, for them and their children, before this gets much, much worse - before they are condemned to who-knows-what ignominy."

"New life, shmoo life!" said Rabbi Elmman. "A life of wandering and desperation, like trees trying to find green places for their roots in a desert! What kind of new life is that? Don't you know what that is? Remember, the President has said these rules are only temporary. How foolish would it be if people flee the U.S. - give up everything - and the temporary rules are then revoked?"

"This, of course, is the same President who created the TAgOp monstrosity," said Stavisky. "And you still believe such a person? And the same Democratic Party that has done nothing to oppose these rules?"

"Many of us believe the President was put up to this - that it is not really the President's idea - that he just did it for political expedience but will take the earliest opportunity to cancel these things!" Rabbi Elmman was emphatic. "Most Democrats know this is not really our party - it is the work of a few zealots."

"I believe," Stavisky said quietly, "that German Jews said the same thing in the mid-1930's - that Hitler's speeches were just for political expediency, just to get elected. Hitler could not really mean what he said. It was the work of a few zealots. It would change after Hitler came to power. This was, after all, Germany, the most civilized nation in the world."

Now it was Rabbi Elmman's turn to be quiet. It was clear that he did not really believe his own words. "So how does this work?" he asked.

Stavisky asked if the Rabbi could think of even one family who might have a different view and would leave if they had the chance.

"Unfortunately, "said the Rabbi, "I know you are right. My congregants may be politically passionate, but most of them are not crazy. Obviously they think about these things. More than a few have told me, confidentially, they would get out if they could. They of course think about Germany."

"So pick a test family," said Stavisky. "If they are interested, I will meet with you and them together and explain the process.

The Rabbi said he would do so, and Stavisky drove back to Boston.

A few days later Stavisky went back to New Hampshire to meet with Rabbi Elmman and Robert and Lillian Smith. Robert was a dentist, Lillian his office manager. They had two teenage daughters, one in public school, the other a student at the famous St. Paul's School in Concord.

Robert told Stavisky they had thought about leaving as soon as the government announced the TAgOp Regs. He said they were lucky because they had a place to go, at least for now - a ski condo in the Laurentians. Also, they had a local bank account there to which they had been transferring funds. They would have enough to live for at least a year, assuming their U.S. bank accounts would be frozen if their flight were discovered. They expected, also, that as a dentist Robert could eke a living wherever they went, even in a black market.

"This is so horrible!" said Lillian, a slightly overweight blonde in her late 40s. "How can we even be talking like this? Eking a living in a black market!" She started to cry.

201

In the end the Smiths decided to go.

Stavisky explained that certain arrangements would be made so that their DNA swipe at the border would not show them as Jews. (He gave no more details because the less they knew the better). They should be ready to leave in a week. When the arrangements were ready, he would telephone the Rabbi, who in turn would call on their landline with a simple message, "Your order is ready." They would then drive to the border, pass the DNA swipe test, and cross into Canada. After they crossed, they would post on Lillian's Facebook page, "The weather is fine." And, for them, the weather would indeed be fine.

There would be no emails or tweets to anyone, not to the Rabbi or Stavisky, and definitely not to their friends or relatives. To avoid alarms in their town, they would tell their friends that they were planning a long-delayed family 'historical trip' around the U.S. - which they wanted to do now before the TAgOp thing got even worse. They would make arrangements with their children's schools for this purpose.

Everything went smoothly. I changed the Smith family's NSA files. One week later Stavisky telephoned the Rabbi, who advised the Smiths, "Your order is ready."

The Smiths were packed and ready to go. Two days later Lillian Smith posted on her Facebook page, "The weather is fine." And they were gone.

35

We had a plan that had worked once. We now had to replicate that success.

The question, also, was how to expand our reach.

To that point we decided to limit the number of departee families to one in each congregation - at least until we were more confident of the process.

We feared that even so small a number would start to trigger rumors. As more and more departee families did not return from "vacation", gossip would certainly begin. And the government would not be far behind.

We were in a window of time that we knew could close very quickly. Sooner rather than later the NSA or ICE would figure out that Jews were beating the system. We had to send off as many Jews as possible before the feds caught on.

In retrospect you will say, of course, that this was impossibly quixotic. Of course it was. But we did it anyway.

We decided to start in the North, near the Canadian border, because crossings by car were the

204

simplest. It should make no difference, of course, if a departee went by car, plane, or train. Yet going through airport security, or even buying a cross-border train ticket, added extra surveillance that could catch us up.

Thus Stavisky began to drive across the northland, contacting Reform rabbis, and I watched the NSA files for hints we were being watched. So far there had been no hint of detection. It may have been dumb luck - or, as I began to wonder, perhaps the hand of Hashem.

When we passed our first 100 departees (actually, 30 families), I told Sarah it was time for her to leave.

It was only a matter of time, I said, before ICE or the NSA found us out. I would not risk having her caught. I wanted her safe in Canada with her parents.

We had a big fight and then made up, with nothing resolved.

We both believed our love was besharet, meaning 'meant to be'. There would never be anyone else for either of us. How could we, so inexperienced and so young, know that? We just did.

We could not face being separated; but, at the same time, I could not face having something bad happen to Sarah.

Then Sarah stunned me. Not only would she <u>not</u> leave; she wanted to do what Stavisky was doing.

She would be a better blind interface, she said, because the world would see only a Chinese girl; no one would think she was Jewish.

Sarah also hit me with another truth. What I was doing, even if a mitzvah, was a drop in the bucket.

Sarah knew, obviously, that Stavisky and I were making it up as we went along. To do more, she said, we would need to come up with a better plan.

Accepting that I could not change her mind about not leaving, and recognizing the truth of what she said, I told her I would think about it. Then, as you will expect, I agreed.

36

Meantime the Jews of America were in more trouble every day.

Jews were scolded on the streets and sometimes roughed up. An Islamic group organized a national "Evict Jews Day" on college campuses; Jewish students awoke one morning to find fake "Eviction Notices" under their dorm room doors.

The stock markets were in a slow, 'dripping-water' decline, a little bit every week.

More and more employers fired Jewish workers without even a pretense of justification. Business owners knew it was the best thing to do to avoid government scrutiny. They did not want the feds asking about Jews on their payroll. Nobody wanted to be on the wrong side of this White House.

In a short time, with Sarah added to the team, we had arranged for more than 225 departees. While this meant only some 60 or so families, communities began to notice they were gone. There were too many Jewish families who took long vacations and did not return.

At this stage there were just the rumors; no one knew for sure whether it was true or how it could be possible. The most repeated story was that Jews were bribing ICE agents at the border. The alleged bribe amounts ranged from $5,000 to $20,000 per person.

Shortly after these rumors started, the media reported that a Jewish family (including their two teen-aged children) had indeed been jailed for trying to bribe ICE agents at the border. The tragic family unfortunately believed the rumors and had tried to act on them. After this event, there were no more rumors of Jews getting out, or trying to get out, through bribery.

Another rumor circulated, however, which did not make the main media. You could allegedly get a new type of "Special Condition Exit Visa" if you donated $500,000 per departee to the Democratic National Committee. Given recent events, most in the Jewish community immediately accepted this rumor as true.

There were also stories of Jewish families trekking across remote wilderness parts of the Canadian border. It was said, also, that ICE was using drones to watch for, and stop, such activity.

Publicity (government sponsored) about ICE arrests and prosecutions apparently did not stop desperate families from continuing these wilderness attempts. (Pundits wrote about the irony of ICE easily interdicting tiny groups on the long, fence-less Canadian border when it could not stop thousands pouring across the easier-watched Mexican border.)

Hadassah AgOp reported all these rumors, along with many others. Although now a voice in the cloud from Canada, my angry mother continued to document the personal hardships of American Jews.

37

One winter afternoon, taking my weekly long walk along the North End wharves, I had another idea. I had been worrying constantly how long it would take for NSA to discover my tampering. How to make my work truly invisible?

The new idea was so simple. I would write a cloaking program to hide my tracks. With such a program no NSA cyber cop, looking for tracks, could find anything. Instead, even after I changed an AgOp file, the original file would appear as before - that is, unchanged.

In other words, even though I would have changed the particular Jew's file, it would appear untouched. (Star Trek fans will know that the idea of "cloaking" was not an original idea - I stole it from Star Trek's brilliant concept of cloaking devices for star ships.)

The cloaking program was easy to write. As with other such things, the mechanics followed the concept.

I finished it in a single all-nighter fueled by black coffee and chocolate chip cookies. The next morning I had a caffeine/sugar hangover and a brilliant program to cover my tracks in saving more Jews. (I figured that the NSA would eventually figure out the cloaking program - but I hoped it would take them a long time.)

With Sarah now joining Stavisky in the cause, we worked day and night. The two of them, like Johnny Appleseed, travelled the roads of America, spreading good seeds, seeds of life, to Jewish families.

Each went separately, of course, meeting quietly with new rabbis in cities and towns across the northern border.

Because in America Jews of all congregations had assimilated names, we had expanded our reach to Conservative and Orthodox congregations. Some of our warmest receptions were from Orthodox rabbis. (It was a fact that the Orthodox had always distrusted political correctness; they had always known that the emperor had no clothes.)

Our protocol was now standard.

Stavisky or Sarah would make an appointment with the rabbi on the pretext of being new in town. They would then have an in-person meeting to explain the procedure. The rabbi would tell them that he or she had to think about it. One day later (sometimes, but rarely, two), the rabbi would call them to come back. They would then discuss the procedure for the departees. The rabbi would give them the names; I would change and then cloak the departees' NSA files; and the departees would cross the border.

In a very short while we passed 500 departees.

With the momentum growing and word getting around the Jewish community, both Stavisky and Sarah began to get unsolicited requests from rabbis and even from prospective departees.

We could never know, of course, whether any call was a government trap. Thus, whenever Sarah or Stavisky received an unplanned call, they denied any knowledge of the program. They then checked out the identity of the caller. If the caller was indeed a rabbi, they then called back to arrange a meeting.

We were all working under incredible pressure, and without much sleep.

Through it all Sarah was amazing. She seemed to have a deep well of quiet strength. Somehow just meeting her eased the anxieties of departee families who were entrusting her with their lives.

Nothing fazed Sarah - not the last minute complications and screw-ups which inevitably happened, not the hardships of days on the road, nothing. She was, as I said, amazing.

Stavisky, however, began to act erratically. Why I did not know; but it became more and more apparent. While he was able to disguise this from his rabbis and departees, I sensed something was wrong. He was, after all, not a young man. I guessed that the pressure was getting to him.

It was time to rethink what we were doing. Clearly we all needed a rest. Now, before we made a mistake or things got away from us, we had to take a break - and we needed to reconsider the safety of Sarah and Stavisky.

Also, since we had known that we could not keep this quiet for long - especially now with hundreds of people touched by the program - we had to have a plan for what happened if and when they found us.

We decided to meet in Cambridge to discuss the situation. Sarah and I asked Stavisky to meet us at our spot by the Charles. We then took a slow walk down the river towards M.I.T.

I said we had to change the plan. One way to do that, I said, would be for Sarah and Stavisky to step back and no longer be the interface with rabbis and departees. Indeed, it would be best if they could become invisible.

We needed to expand the team. We had to do that anyway, I said, if we were to grow the program. With just the two of them we were limiting our reach and exhausting them. It was bad project management. We needed new team members.

"But who can we trust?" Sarah asked. "And who could we possibly ask? It's a huge sacrifice! To join us means you put life and property at risk - and the lives of your loved ones!"

Stavisky wanted time to think about it. I suggested we each make a list of people we might ask and meet again in two days.

One surprising answer came unsolicited, however.

The day after our river walk there came a knock on my door. It was Ari!

"Nu!" he said when I opened the door. "I understand this is Resistance Central! I'm here to resist!"

I hugged him like a long lost brother. "Why are you here? Are you nuts? Why did you come back? Are you crazy?" I was speechless.

"I'm like the Rabbi's mice before their bar mitzvah!" he said. "I can't stay away from the Shul!"

He said he had been following all the stories about Jews leaving, or trying to leave. He decided that he had to be part of that process. So he had travelled from the Caribbean to Canada and then simply had taken a train into the U.S.

"They weren't doing DNA swipes for people coming in!" he joked. "What Jewish boy, once out, would ever come back?"

"Whatever they are saying here," he continued, "all the Jews in Canada talk about is what they call the 'ExUs' - meaning the Exodus of the Jews from the U.S. By now everyone knows someone who has come over. And they whisper about some mythical superhero/magician who is helping departees. Some of them call him my name, the "un-Mohel", because he turns Jews into gentiles!"

He laughed. "So I ask myself - who could be such a person, this un-Mohel? Do I know anyone who could do that? And, after long and careful thought - maybe one second, I remind myself of course that it is you - even if you hadn't started with my family. They are fine, by the way; and they say a blessing for you every day."

"But why come back?" I asked. "We got you out. Why come back?"

"Why <u>not</u> come back?" Ari said. "I am - someday - going to be a doctor. What do doctors do?

They save lives, right. Right now there are a lot of lives that need saving. So why would I not start here?"

He gave me a look of great force. Something in him had changed. While he could still joke about the Rabbi's mice, he was now a man. Both Sarah and I saw in him a strength we had not seen before.

"So what do I do?" he asked.

The answer was simple. We made him the leader of our new "Second Team". We called Stavisky to join us at the apartment and spent the rest of that day with Ari and Stavisky planning the new campaign.

Putting together the Second Team took less time than we expected. In short order we added three other members - a Harvard girl who was a friend of Sarah's; a boy who had been a Lord of Hack the year ahead of me at Stuyvesant; and a friend of Ari from his Yeshiva years, who was now non-observant yet passionately Jewish.

38

Before sending our Second Team into country we decided to pause for thirty days. We wanted to drill our new colleagues in the precise procedures we had developed. We wanted to see, also, what, if any, news or rumors circulated about the prior departees.

Stavisky and Sarah took this time to organize their files about the rabbis they had contacted and the departees they had helped.

It was risky to keep such incriminating data; but we thought it might be of historical importance. So we kept no paper files. Instead we saved the data on two thumb drives which Sarah and Stavisky each kept separately in a safe places known only to them.

Since they would no longer be the field commandos, Sarah and Stavisky were now our command central. Each would be the strategist for two members of the Second Team, coordinating communications through Ari.

Sarah and Stavisky would also be our intelligence apparatchiks, watching the internet and media for hints we were being tracked. In addition, they would watch for stories of Jews escaping (or trying to do so); and would monitor government actions against Jews throughout the country.

There was no lack of news. Sarah and Stavisky continually found rumors about escape attempts of all kinds. They found, also, many stories about Christians helping Jewish families to depart. In fact, a new "Underground Railroad" - now dubbed the "Israel Express" - was developing, organized at first by Evangelical Christians but soon expanded to and by Americans of many backgrounds.

Sarah and Stavisky found nothing, however, not even a hint, to show we were being watched.

As for government actions, they found too much. The Jews of America were under siege.

Thousands had lost their jobs or their professional licenses for "legal compliance". Federal, state, and local agencies now declared Jews ineligible to receive unemployment insurance, social security, food stamps, or other public assistance. Jews were the target of every kind of official investigation and enforcement action.

The Treasury issued proposed regulations to disqualify AgOps from participating in pension plans, IRAs, and 401(k) plans. Older Jews feared that they would soon lose their Social Security benefits.

All these things followed with perverse logic, of course, from the original premise of the TAgOp Regs. Once a government taints a particular group or class of people, why should that group or class have some rights but not others? If Jews had no right to practice a profession, why should they have a right to unemployment insurance?

All major Jewish organizations were now united in purpose, if not in method.

Some Jewish leaders believed the only hope was to contest the TAgOp structure in the courts. The America of the Founders, they argued, the America that embraced all and allowed all to flourish, must be legally restored. They filed a constitutional challenge that was now in federal court in Los Angeles.

Other Jewish leaders argued that the only real choice was departure, not restoration. Skeptical of a good outcome in the courts, they said only political pressure could open the borders. Here they had the strong support of the American people, a majority of whom favored allowing the Jews to leave (and, if possible, rescinding the TAgOp Regs).

A third group of Jewish leaders argued for self-help. They said political pressure would not work with an Imperial Presidency; and what if the Supreme Court held the TAgOp structure to be constitutional? The handwriting was on the wall in big, bright letters - what happened in Germany must not be allowed again! Every Jew should try to get out as soon as possible by any available means.

39

It was at this time, during our 30-day hiatus, during the great debate of Jewish leaders in the media, that Sarah received a strange visit.

Sarah had arranged her course schedule to take large lecture courses so she would not be missed in class and she could do catch-up reading later. Luckily for her, our 30-day hiatus coincided with Reading Period. To be quiet and away from my pacing and coffee, she had decided to study in her room in Lowell House.

One morning, taking a break from her reading, Sarah took a walk to Mt. Auburn Street. She wanted to stretch her legs and get a cup of coffee. It was early January, a grey Cambridge winter day.

As Sarah stopped at a curb, waiting for the 'walk' signal, a man approached her and said he needed directions. He had a slight Israeli accent.

"I think I'm lost," he said. "Can you help me?"

Since it was a public place and he seemed like a tourist, Sarah asked where he wished to go.

"Canada," he said.

Sarah was electrified. "I...I'm not sure what you mean?" she said.

"I think you do," said the stranger. "Please. Do not be afraid. I am a friend. Join me for a cup of coffee."

Scared, Sarah had to choose in a second between flight and agreement.

She did not run. Something about the stranger told her there was no danger. She thought, also, that she had to find out more about anyone who seemed to know about the program.

Taking a breath, Sarah suggested they go to Au Bon Pain on Mass. Avenue. It was a large coffee shop-bakery where two people having coffee would not be noticed.

"My name is Menachem," said the stranger, after they were seated with two espressos, "although sometimes my name is Joe. And you, of course, are the woman we call the "Chinese Maideleh".

"We?"

"Your friends in Israel, of course," said Menachem.

"I didn't know I had friends in Israel," said Sarah.

"Of course you do," said Menachem. "Not too many, but very well-placed I assure you. We have been following your excellent work with the departees."

"I have no idea what you are talking about," said Sarah.

"Perhaps not. Or perhaps so. Let us "assume for discussion", as I believe they say at Harvard, that you do know what I am talking about. In such event, please hear me out." He took a sip of espresso.

Sarah looked at him closely. He seemed in his late thirties or early forties. He was about five-ten, with dark hair and eyes. He wore a white, open-collared shirt and European-style jacket in the Israeli fashion.

"Let us also say, for discussion, that you -and perhaps one other person - for discussion, let us say a Harvard professor - have been travelling the country and contacting rabbis." Menachem spoke in a calm, low voice so as not to be overheard at nearby tables.

"And then, also for discussion, let us say that after you contact these rabbis, Jewish families somehow walk across the border and are not stopped! For them the Red Sea has parted. A miracle!" Menachem smiled.

223

"But how do you do this miracle? How do you part the Red Sea? It is fascinating indeed. For discussion, of course." He took another sip of espresso.

"I deny everything you say," said Sarah. "You, a stranger, approach me on the street with wild accusations! I am just a Harvard student! Why am I even talking to you?"

"Why, indeed? But you are talking to me. You, a Harvard student whose parents are now in Canada," said Menachem.

Sarah started to get up. She was scared. "I have no idea who you are," she said. "What you are saying is outrageous! Why should I believe a word you say?"

"Because you need friends," Menachem said. "You and whoever else are doing this. And believe me, we are your friends. I am Mossad. We want to help you and protect you. We must save as many as we can. Remember, "Never Again!"

"How can you prove what you say?" Sarah asked - "if, somehow, I am who you say I am - which I deny absolutely!"

"Let's say I can figure out a way to do that," said Menachem. "What we want to know is how you do it."

"How we do it?" asked Sarah.

"How you do it,'" said Joe.

"Suppose even I don't know the answer to that question?" said Sarah.

"We can still help and protect you - and whoever it is who knows the answer to that question - this "un-Mohel", as some call him," said Menachem. "You see, we know that he exists - this person who transforms Jews into non-Jews! We are amazed at him!"

He finished his espresso. "Please consider this - we can watch over your shoulder. We can look around corners for you. We can be your eyes and ears - and perhaps more. You need protection. You need our technical support. We can help! We want to help!"

"Can you out-spy the U.S. government?" Sarah asked.

"I do not need to answer that," said Menachem. "But trust me - we can do what we can do! I will be back in touch after you get validation of what I have told you."

"How will I get that?" asked Sarah.

"You will see," said Menachem. And he stood up and strolled casually down Mass. Ave., looking in the shop fronts.

It started to rain, lightly. Sarah walked to our apartment in the rain in a state of shock.

40

"It had to happen," I said when she told me. "Something like this. If this really is Mossad, it is so much better than the feds. And we should have thought that Israel might be watching. We should have thought indeed. Look what is happening between the two governments!"

I have not yet mentioned how the TAgOp regime had electrified Israelis.

Unlike anything in Israel's history, even the Intifadas - even Iran getting the bomb after their deal with the Obama Administration - Part Two had unified all Israeli voices, from extreme Orthodox to far Left. Israelis now worked publicly and privately to oppose Part Two in every way they could and also to help American Jews however they could.

Part Two had also had an immediate impact on Israel. It formally ended the special relationship Israel had so long had with the United States and, bluntly, the end of any notion that the U.S. would defend Israel if attacked by Iran or an Arab country. How could the U.S. justify defending a country of AgOps?

The un-wind had started with Barack Obama, who pretended he would help Israel but in fact did the opposite. Now it was complete.

Indeed, shortly after issuance of the Part Two Regs, the President said the U.S. was "evaluating" its relationship and treaties with Israel in light of the "historic record of oppression of Victims by Agents of Oppression which is now coming to light."

When the Prime Minister of Israel requested an emergency meeting with the President to discuss the TAgOp Regs, the President put him off. The formal reason was the President's unforgiving schedule for the next six months; but both parties knew the real reason.

The Prime Minister then called an emergency meeting of his own Cabinet to start planning for worst-case scenarios. "One thing is clear," said the Prime Minister. "If we were not alone in the world before, we are now."

As happened, this was not quite true. A small but surprising number of countries issued formal protests to the U.S. about the TAgOp Regs and Part Two. These included, among others, Canada, Australia, New Zealand, and - surprisingly, Germany. They voted to support Israel's motion in the U.N. General Assembly calling on the U.S. to rescind the TAgOp rules. Like any

U.N. proposal by or favoring Israel, of course, the motion was overwhelmingly defeated.

Now Sarah and I sat watching the rain fall on Cambridge and considering how Mossad could help us.

It was very clear, also, that time was running out. If Mossad had found us, the feds would, too.

We had to use our remaining time to 'depart' as many Jews as possible.

Five days later Sarah received a weird letter from her father. (I note that we often used snail mail to communicate.) While NSA could open letters, we had no evidence it had started to do so - perhaps because paper mail had become a curiosity used mainly by old people and advertisers trying to reach them. Snail mail meant three or more days extra between messages. But we were trying to minimize risk.

(When communicating with rabbis, if snail mail was too slow, we used landlines and burn phones - never the internet.)

The weird letter said that Sarah's parents had been visited by Menachem, a distant cousin of Ruth Po, and that they were thrilled so see him. They had not known he existed; but his great grandfather was the brother of Sarah's great grandfather. He was thus a member of the family.

"All that means is that they contacted your family, too," I said. "It's not proof."

"No, but it means my parents think he is real," said Sarah.

Since we knew now that someone claiming to be Mossad was watching us, we decided not to meet in public any more - and also that Sarah and Stavisky should not be seen together any more.

We had one last meeting together - Sarah, Ari, Stavisky, and I - to discuss the roll out of the Second Team.

With Mossad - if, indeed, that is who they were - watching, we had no time to lose. Sending four new faces into the field would increase our impact, however slowly and incrementally. But we needed to get going. We needed to get more people out and more quickly.

We decided that Ari and his three cohorts would fan across the country, seeking new rabbis and departees. The plan was to crisscross the land, targeting inland areas as well as border regions. Jews in the midland might be less suspect to anyone watching us. However, they would then have to figure out ways to reach the borders.

Stavisky and I chatted for a few moments about my forays through the NSA. He knew, of course, about the 'back-door key' that I used to gain access. I had not told him before about the cloaking program, however. He was fascinated.

"You mean someone looking at the file sees it unchanged - even though you changed it?" Stavisky asked.

"Exactly," I said.

"How do you do it?" he asked.

"Next time we have time to talk, I'll explain it," I said. "Meanwhile I think it is why they haven't found me yet. Otherwise who can explain it? Not even a sign they are watching!"

Stavisky gave me a funny look.

The end of our meeting was emotional. We were not sure when we would all be together again. We knew, however, that the world was changing faster than we could keep pace.

41

With the situation of American Jews more dire each day, we worked under constant time pressure. Our Second Team fanned across the country as planned. Thus far our plan was working; every week we helped more and more Jewish families to cross the border.

We began to hear rumors of a fierce debate in the White House, with each of two factions leaking stories to the media.

The first faction, led by the Treasury Secretary, said that Jews must be allowed to go - in fact, must be expelled. The Jews were a cancer in America, they argued. They must be removed as quickly as possible. Keeping them in limbo, keeping them in the country but outside society, they said, was killing the economy. Besides, argued this faction, keeping them was creating a climate of hatred unlike any in American history. This must not be allowed to last - who knew where it would end?

The American people, said the Treasury Secretary, would not permit a Holocaust within their borders (even if they had accepted an equivalent of the Nazi Nuremberg Laws.) So, argued the Treasury Secretary, we must expel them. "We must follow the example of Spain in 1492; no good will come of keeping them here."

The second group, led by the President's National Security Advisor, refused to consider letting the Jews leave. This group insisted the Jews must be made to pay.

"We want our pound of flesh!" said the National Security Advisor. "They must feel the pain! Maybe after the Jews have paid in full for past sins, the "special status" could be revoked. The Jews could then be restored to their former places under the Victims Law, like everyone else. If you let them leave, what message would that send? It would admit to the world that we have treated them unjustly!"

According to rumor, the President was indecisive and needed more time to decide. Since the President held all power, neither faction could prevail.

The result of this stalemate - unreported but known to everyone through leak and rumor - was that, for now, the Jews would not be allowed to go - but perhaps later.

It was a time of desperate waiting for American Jews. They tried to go about their lives, coping with the daily inflictions of Part Two while they hoped against hope that the first group would prevail and the gates would open.

How, then, I asked Sarah, can we get more departees out even faster?

Sarah and I had, of course, stopped going out together in public. When we went out alone, we always looked over our shoulders to see if we were watched.

Reading Period ended for Sarah, and there was a huge blizzard, the worst to hit Boston in years.

In a holiday mood because of the storm, we decided we had to get out, and devil the consequences. So we took the "T" to downtown Boston and walked to O'Pietro in the North End.

The place was open, but, because of the storm, we were the only customers. We sat down, ordered a bottle of Chianti, and began to look at the menus.

A man entered. When he removed his hat and coat, Sarah kicked me. It was Menachem. He asked to be seated at the table next to us.

"Hello again," he said to Sarah. "I am your long-lost cousin - as I think your parents have told you. It is so nice to see you again. And who is your friend?"

We said nothing.

"We really should speak," he said, "because we have a common family problem. Our family is so big.

We would like to send everyone on a vacation reunion. But we can't figure out how to get everyone to the same place at the same time. We thought you might have an answer - or that you are thinking of the same problem."

Sarah and I were silent.

Then he said, "It would help the cause if we knew how you do it." He spoke to Sarah but looked at me. "We know the person who does this is a math genius. We think he may actually be the one. But how could we know?"

"And how would you do it?" I asked.

"Aha!" he said. "A sign of interest. Perhaps I am not in the wrong place after all." He ordered a glass of Chianti and a salad from the hovering waitress. "I show you mine and then you show me yours?" he said.

"It depends on what you show us," I said.

"I will let my boss show you," said Menachem.

And that is how we came to meet the head of Mossad.

We actually met two people - the head of Mossad, whose name was Uri ben Moishe, and his top aide, a woman named Rachel Levin. Uri was a movie version of the head of Mossad - about 60, distinguished, a full head of grey hair, piercing eyes. Which perhaps should have tipped me off.

Rachel was not a movie version of anything - slight, with scholar spectacles, dark hair, indifferent of dress. You would not have looked twice at her.

We met at a house in Vermont, near the Canadian border. We followed the GPS directions Menachem gave us to a meadow surrounded by forest. Edging the forest was a 1960s-era chalet, like many which defined Vermont ski areas after World War II.

There was no one around, except two moose grazing in the distance.

How Uri and Rachel got there we never found out.

After introductions and an offer of tea, which we declined, Uri got down to business.

"We know you are getting people out. We do not know how. And we know that you are limited. You can only do a few at a time. And, of course, we know that you will eventually be caught. If we found you, so will the NSA."

"And how did you find us?" I asked.

236

"You think we would not find out with all these Jews crossing to Canada?" Uri joked. "Departees talk. Rabbis talk. They talk to each other. Some of them talk to us - even though they do not know it is us to whom they are talking. Word speeds around."

Uri stared at us. "Did you think you could make dozens - hundreds - of Jewish families take long vacations - and never come back - and not have people talk? You have been very lucky the NSA or DHS have not caught on. Very, very lucky! But we still can't figure out how you do it."

Sarah and I sat silently. Then I said, "Assuming you are right, why are we here?"

"Two reasons," said Uri. "If you and we join forces, we have resources which can increase your output. And we have our own plan – a different approach – which perhaps you can help us with."

"What is your plan?" I asked quietly.

"It is the simplest of plans," said Uri. "We do what Moses did. We go to Pharaoh and demand that Pharaoh let our people go."

"Just like that?" I asked.

"Not quite just like that, of course," said Uri. "But a modified 'just like that'".

"How modified?" I asked.

"Modified with a lever," said Uri. "Modified to be an offer they can't refuse."

I looked out the window. The two moose were still grazing across the meadow.

"Which is where you come in," said Uri. "We think your special gifts may help us find the lever we need. So please tell us how you do it."

Something told me not to divulge my secret; so I answered a question with a question. "Have your hackers penetrated the NSA?" I asked.

Uri hesitated. My simple question had unsettled the head of Mossad.

"I am not sure I can answer that question," he said. "It could endanger you."

"And I have the same answer to your question," I said. "If I tell you, it could endanger you - as well as us."

I looked at Sarah, who indicated "no" with the very slightest flicker of an eyelid.

Uri looked at Rachel Levin, who said, quietly, "So there we are. So there we are indeed. But perhaps, for now, neither of us needs to know the 'how'. We need only to work together."

Rachel's words seemed to settle the issue.

"So," said Uri, "you will not tell us how, and we will not tell you about our non-hackers - at least for now. But let us begin working together. We will coordinate together. There will come a day - soon - when the U.S. will open its borders - when the Jews of America will walk out the front door - and you will be a key factor. But please think how you can help us."

I was curious. "How could I possibly help?"

"You make a miracle each time you send out a family of departees," said Uri. "We don't know how - but we know it is you. If you can make such a miracle, perhaps you can make other miracles."

"And what kind of miracles would you like me to make?" I asked.

"Do you remember how God persuaded Pharaoh to let our people go?"

"Plagues!" said Sarah.

"Plagues," said Uri.

He looked at me. "Precisely. Plagues. We want you to help us make plagues - to persuade the American Pharaoh to let our people go."

I thought he might smile; he did not. "Not blood plagues, or locusts, or boils. Of course not! Instead - computer plagues! Computer plagues that disrupt everyday life! Computer plagues that create popular outcry to let the Jews go! But reversible plagues, of course. We do not wish to do permanent harm."

Uri shook his head sadly. "We will always love America for what it was. For the America to which Jews came and, in liberty, thrived. We love the American people. We just want this President to let our people go."

I was stunned.

"And who is your Moses?" I asked.

"We do not know yet," said Uri. (At least he was honest.) "But he will appear. We know he will appear."

I shook my head in disbelief.

"You said you would show me something at this meeting. What have you shown me?" I asked.

Uri was thoughtful. "We have shown you who we are and what we plan to do. And now we ask - we ask with open hearts - that you help us."

"You <u>must</u> do this!" said Rachel. "You are the one who can do this."

"Think about it," said Uri. "These things <u>must</u> be done. While they cannot be achieved overnight, yet neither can we take too long." He stood up to leave, and Rachel with him. "We will be back in touch."

"Here is a safe land line number," said Rachel, handing me a piece of paper. "Just in case you need us before we contact you again. Just leave a voice mail saying, "It's time to do lunch." Then go the next evening at 6 p.m. to the restaurant where you met Menachem. He will be there. If he is not there when you arrive, wait ten minutes, then leave."

"Now we must be going," said Uri. "By the way, this house is rented for the weekend, if you two would like to stay."

"And one last thing," said Rachel. "We will have people watching out for you. You will not see them. But they will not be far. Just in case."

And the meeting ended.

Uri and Rachel left first. At their request, we waited an hour. Then we, too, left. We did not want to stay the weekend in that house.

So Mossad would watch our every move from now on. How soon would others catch on?

42

Our Second Team flourished.

Ari joked that instead of becoming a doctor he should have been a community organizer. It was a good way to meet nice Jewish girls, including one hot unmarried woman rabbi with whom he spent a lovely evening in Denver. Her name was Naomi Goldman. From the way he spoke we thought she might be more than just a lovely evening.

Each week we 'departed' about 75 families - usually 200-300 people. Each of our four "representatives" visited at least one rabbi every day or two.

Most rabbis were now expectant. All knew, through the grapevine, about the departee 'program'. Many already had lists prepared of families who would go.

We began to get repeat business, also, from rabbis with whom we had worked earlier. They reached out to Sarah and Stavisky through coded snail mail.

As we sent out more and more departees, conditions worsened every day for American Jews.

A great majority of Americans protested the TAgOp Regs and defended their Jewish friends. Others, however, became persecutors or at least social anti-Semites. Jews found themselves shunned in the workplace, or by former friends, or in social settings. Bullying of Jewish children at school was an everyday thing.

Campus and Islamist groups who earlier agitated for Israel BDS now pushed for "American Jew BDS."

They demanded that Americans boycott Jewish businesses and professionals and divest investment from Jewish-controlled companies. They demanded tougher sanctions of all kinds against Jews far beyond Part Two.

Jews were frozen out of jobs in government, academia, or with non-profit organizations. Jewish homes sold at big discounts because buyers guessed the owners had to sell to raise cash (whether to survive or in hopes of leaving).

There were now Jewish homeless on the streets.

Sarah and I had told no one about our meeting with Mossad.

Then, when Ari returned briefly to Cambridge to report on his efforts, we had dinner in our apartment.

Mid-way through dinner I decided to tell him about the meeting with Mossad.

I wanted Ari's perspective. Also, I thought it was vital that he know because Mossad was obviously watching him, too.

In short order Sarah and I recounted the whole history with Mossad, beginning with her first meeting with Menachem.

Ari was delighted. Only good could come of a partnership with Mossad, he said. He was particularly interested in the idea of computer plagues.

"Imagine," he said, "suppose an American Moses went to Pharaoh and threatened plagues! What would be the response?"

It was a question with many possible answers.

The President and this Administration were deeply invested in the TAgOp regime. It was difficult to think that a threat of plagues, let alone the reality of computer plagues, would do more than harden their resolve.

But who could say if the American people might not rise up and demand that the President open the gates?

There were many possibilities.

"You said Mossad thinks it will work," said Ari. "And remember," he joked, "it worked once before! Hashem hardened Pharaoh's heart, then made him relent!"

He became thoughtful. "What kind of computer plagues could you think of?"

Since the meeting with Mossad I had, in fact, been thinking of exactly that. What plagues indeed could I think of?

I had been mulling over three possible ideas.

I described each plague to Ari in some detail. He listened intently, as if memorizing them.

"Do you really think you could do <u>any</u> of those?" he asked.

Each would take some doing, I said. Each was differently complex. But <u>all</u> had a common problem. All of them would require perfectly timed execution.

To launch each plague I would have to get in and out of the target servers in twenty minutes or risk certain detection.

Ari was obviously fascinated. "Definitely keep planning!" he said. "Right now you think they are academic. But you must be ready. You are the only one who can do this. And you never know when Moses may come calling!"

"And where is this Moses who will call on me to create his plagues?" I asked.

"Mossad told you God would provide a Moses," Ari said.

"Not exactly," I said. "Mossad said they believed a Moses would appear. But they were clearly not as sure as you are!"

"Keep planning those plagues," said Ari. "You never know. I have a feeling in my bones."

"Hineni," I joked.

Ari looked at me and said nothing.

43

Ari went back to his travels, and I went back to changing Jews into non-Jews in the NSA files.

Every few days I did a pass through the files just for reconnaissance. For each pass I used a different starting point from the greynet, cloaked by my cloaking program. I wanted to see if anyone else was walking these forests - other than the usual NSA data-types.

In all the months in the NSA files I had not met another explorer. Yet, two days after the dinner with Ari, I met my first.

The intruder did not see me behind the cloaking program.

Sipping my morning coffee, I watched the screen. How the intruder gained access was not clear; the intruder was very clumsy, appearing to check random Victim files with no obvious pattern.

Then something weird happened.

As I watched, an NSA 'watching' program caught and trapped the intruder - then ejected it from the NSA files.

The intruder's entry was deleted; but not before I traced the intruder to a URL address in Los Angeles.

So the NSA did have internal monitoring, after all! Had I had just been smart enough - or lucky enough - not to get caught?

I watched for signs of punitive action. Did the feds identify the intruder? If so, would there be a public arrest? Or was this something they would keep quiet?

Sure enough, two days later I found a one-paragraph story in the LA Times. It said that the FBI had arrested an AgOp man (they never said "Jew") for allegedly hacking government files. The man's name was Jonah Isaacs. The story said the FBI had not yet determined the man's motive.

Needless to say, I wanted to know more about Mr. Isaacs and what happened to him.

I decided it would be crazy, however, to probe. I did not want my fingerprints anywhere near the Isaacs incident. Also, what if the whole thing were a trap? What if the NSA had created the whole thing - including Isaacs' clumsy hack - to trap me, or someone like me? I confined myself to watching media reports for more details.

Then I had a better idea. I called the Mossad phone number and said it was time to do lunch.

The next evening Menachem was waiting at O'Pietro when Sarah and I arrived. We took our place at the table next to his.

"Always a pleasure!" said Menchem. "You two have not aged a bit since we last met."

"Not us," I said. "But perhaps someone else has." I asked if any of his friends had been arrested recently - perhaps in Los Angeles.

Menachem did not even hesitate. "You know," he said, "we were going to ask you the same question. We saw that story about -what was his name, Isaacs? Do you know, we thought it might have to do with you. Then we thought - never! It could never have to do with you - what could you possibly be doing in the NSA files?" He smirked.

"Who said anything about the NSA files?" I asked. "The newspapers didn't say that!"

"It was just my random guess," said Menachem. He sipped his Chianti.

"So Mr. Isaacs, whatever he was doing, was not one of yours?"

"No." He added simply, "Ours do not get caught."

"And what do you know about Mr. Isaacs?" I asked.

"Strangely," said Menachem, "Mr. Isaacs does not appear to exist."

Now I was the one who took some Chianti.

"That explains the clumsiness," I said, speaking before I thought not to.

"Clumsiness?" said Menachem. "What clumsiness?" He looked at me with interest.

I changed the subject. "How is your plague-planning going?" I asked.

"Ah, our plague planning," he said.

"And who will be Moses?" asked Sarah.

"Good questions," said Menachem. "Very good questions indeed. We have the idea for some plagues, but no one to execute them." He looked at Sarah. "And, as for Moses, well - we hope God will make him appear to us."

"Would not Moses himself execute the plagues?" Sarah asked.

"No," said Menachem. "Moses was great leader but no computer hacker. Besides, if you remember your Torah, it was God - not Moses - who sent the plagues."

"Don't you have great hackers?" I asked. "Israel invented the internet!"

"Of course we do! Of course!" said Menachem. "The best in the world - except for one. That one"- and he looked fixedly at me -"that one is the guy freeing the departees! That one is the guy we need to execute the plagues!"

"I think we both should learn more about the non-existent Mr. Isaacs," I said. "Why would the FBI announce they had caught a non-existent computer hacker?"

"Why indeed?" said Menachem. "Of course we should learn more about Mr. Isaacs. But that is a diversion. It should not stop you from helping with the plagues."

"What are they, these plagues of yours?" I asked.

He described the two plagues.

"Banal," I said. "Those two will never change the mind of Pharaoh."

At the President's direction, State "temporarily" suspended all relations with Israel. It was a temporary suspension, rather than a termination, said the Secretary of State, because appropriate final resolution of this matter was "still under study".

Israel was allowed to keep its embassy in Washington and its mission to the U.N; but it had to close all consulates in the U.S. Travel between Israel and the U.S was interdicted except for diplomats and those with special visas.

It was a classic action for a cunning President who always hedged a bet.

The Ninth Circuit decision was not just a death knell for Jewish hopes. To all Americans of conscience it was the end of any illusion of America as a free society.

For the next two months, despite the Ninth Circuit decision, our "Second Wave" continued in the ordinary course, traveling the roads of a grim America.

Rabbis were contacted; departees were identified; I changed NSA files, and the departees made their exits - most by car, but some by air or train. Everyone on our team knew this was a calm before the storm. How or what that storm would be, and how torrential, we could not know.

I continued to work on the three plagues that I had described to Menachem and Ari.

I also considered but rejected a few other ideas - such as replicating an electromagnetic pulse attack to shut down the U.S. power grid. I would have turned the power back on, of course, after the U.S. let the Jews leave. But the unintended consequences of such a hack were beyond imagining. I could not do it.

Another issue Sarah and I discussed was whether to threaten a plague first and then negotiate with the President - or do the plague first and negotiate after. (I would not be the negotiator, of course - that must be our Moses, whoever he might be.)

Negotiating first would give the President time to try to thwart the plague and find the plague-maker, meaning me. Not good planning. So the tactic must be plague first, negotiation second.

Sarah and I thought, perhaps, that the Prime Minister of Israel would be our Moses.

Sudden events then answered these questions in ways we could not have predicted.

45

The end started with a loud banging on my door.

I was sitting at the computers with my first morning coffee. I rushed to the door. "Who is it?" I yelled.

"Menachem! Quick! Open up!"

I opened the door to a harried Menachem, who pushed into the room. "You must leave now!" he said. "Take whatever you need for your work! Leave everything else! Don't ask questions! I'll explain later! We must hurry!"

I looked at the table with my computers. I would take my laptop and comp-pad.

"We must destroy everything!" I said. Those computers must not fall into NSA hands!

"How can you do that - and fast?" asked Menachem.

I had long planned for this possibility. I could not know when it might come. Yet it was an obvious first-tier contingency that had to be anticipated.

I had three desktop computers that could not come with me. All three were linked in a self-destruct program that would render the hard-drives impossible to recover.

Surprised at how calm I was, I started the coded self-destruct sequence. In a few seconds my computers would be junk.

"Quickly!" said Menachem.

I took a last look around the apartment that had been our refuge of togetherness.

"Sarah!" I yelled. "What about Sarah? She went to class!"

"We are trying to find her," said Menachem. "But we can discuss that on the way. Now we must go! And quickly!" he repeated.

I put my laptop and comp-pad in my backpack, then followed Menachem out the door and down the fire stairs.

Waiting at the curb was a non-descript blue van with its back door open. Menachem motioned me through the door, then followed and pulled the door shut behind him.

Recovering from the shock of these events, I looked around the van. I was stunned. Each wall of the van, as well as each rear door, had a large window not visible from the outside. This was not your grandfather's plumber van.

Even as the van pulled out into Mass. Avenue, two black SUVs swung in behind us. Out jumped five or six men in SWAT gear, who then rushed into my building.

"DHS!" said Menachem. "We guessed right! And, as you Americans say, just in the nick of time!"

I was still in shock and trying to absorb all this. "What did you guess? And where is Sarah?" I asked. "Where is Sarah?"

"Sarah first," said Menachem. "We have a team looking for her. Where did she say she was going?"

"First to class. Then to her mailbox at Rent-A-Box," I said. "She went every morning to see if she had mail from our Second Team."

I realized that Menachem might not know about our Second Team.

"Your Second Team is why we thought DHS would come after you. That was our correct guess."

Menachem shook his head sadly. "Three members of your Second Team have been arrested."

"How did you know about the Second Team?" I asked.

"Do you think we would not know of your Second Team? Remember who we are!" said Menachem. "It was because we were watching that we learned of the arrests - although we didn't know until now that you call them the 'Second Team'."

"What happened?" I asked.

"As you might guess, we were monitoring DHS email traffic. Last night we saw emails about an operation to arrest four people suspected of helping TAgOps escape."

Menachem shook his head. "The emails said the four were contacting rabbis and arranging somehow for TAgOps to cross the border. There were to be simultaneous arrests in Maine, Colorado, Texas, and Florida."

"But you said only three were arrested," I said.

"Right," said Menachem. "Apparently they couldn't get the fourth."

I wondered who had been caught and who not. Where was Ari?

"Where are they now?" I asked.

"They are being taken to a secret DHS compound in Virginia. That's all we could get from the e-mails."

I wanted to warn the fourth, who would know nothing of what had happened.

I told Menachem I needed to send an email. It would be a blind email from a cloaked source saying simply, "18!" It was a protocol we had long planned with the Second Team against such a possibility.

Menachem didn't like the idea. "If they track it back to you, they will find us," he said.

"Let's find an internet café. I can send it from there. They will know the location but nothing else."

Menachem turned and spoke in Hebrew to the driver. The van continued down Mass. Ave and across the Charles into Boston, where it turned up Commonwealth Avenue until it came to a stop in front of a small student internet café.

"Make it fast!" said Menachem.

I jumped from the van and walked quickly into the café. I did not want to pay with a credit card and instead paid cash for 15 minutes of time. I sat down at a computer and quickly typed out my message. It would go not just to the Second Team, but also to Sarah and Stavisky.

What about Stavisky? In the rush to escape I had forgotten about Stavisky!

Back in the van I asked Menachem if Mossad had been watching Stavisky.

I remembered that, at our first meeting, Menachem had told Sarah they had been watching her and a Harvard professor's interactions with rabbis. So they clearly knew about Stavisky.

Menachem said they had indeed been watching Stavisky. This morning, however, he had eluded them.

"He may have thought it was your DHS," said Menachem. "He is a wily old fox who grew up in the Soviet Union. I am sure he knows one or two things about being watched, and watching the watchers, and disappearing."

I regretted not telling Stavisky about Mossad. I had thought it would be more dangerous for him if he knew. It was clearly a mistake. I hoped it would not prove serious.

At least when Stavisky got the "18" he would know to become invisible.

The blue van now drove uneventfully to an old estate down on the South Shore. There was a main house and a cluster of three red barns and a shed. Old trees surrounded the house and lined the long driveway. It was a good place to be unobtrusive. The van pulled into one of the barns.

Inside the house was an emergency, but world-class, computer/communications set-up. Mossad had certainly been doing advance planning.

Where to start first? We had to find Sarah and Stavisky. We had to find out which three were arrested and who was not. In the press of such matters I forgot about my work on the three plagues.

Our first answer to one of these questions came from a bizarre source - YouTube.

Two hours after we arrived at the estate a Mossad tech, one of several who were watching the computer screens, gave out a yell in Hebrew. Everyone rushed over to see what was happening.

The tech was an attractive woman with dark hair, dark eyes, and a tight-fitting black tee shirt and trousers. She said something in Hebrew, then changed to English when she saw me. "Look!" she said. "Isn't he one of your team?"

I looked at the screen. It was Ari!

He was standing in a large room with plain white walls. On the wall behind him was an American flag. For reasons I did not know then, he was dressed all in white, with a white kippah on his head.

"Yes! His name is Ari Cohen!" I said. "But what is he doing?"

The tech hit a key to play the video. This was Ari's speech:

"This is a message for the President of the United States."

"My name is Ari Cohen. If you want to verify this, I am a pre-med sophomore at Harvard. If you are watching this video, something terrible has happened to me and my friends."

"My friends and I have been helping Jewish families to depart the United States. The Government says this is illegal; we say it is moral and just."

"For those moral and just actions, my friends have now been arrested, probably by the Department of Homeland Security - the American Secret Police. I say "probably" because I do not know exactly. This video was to be released on my instructions if one or more of us was arrested."

"The Jews of America are being held prisoners in our own land. We thought we were Americans."

"Our parents or grandparents came here, many of them, as penniless refugees, drawn by the American dream. And it was not just a dream – it was real."

"They worked hard and prospered. And they gave back in every possible way."

"But now we are told they and we were never real Americans. No, those penniless refugees who worked so hard and gave back so much, were oppressors, historic evildoers."

"The government has created a fraudulent history to cast our forefathers and us as villains who are responsible for every American ill."

"The government has imposed punishments on us which are clearly illegal and unconstitutional, even if a corrupt judiciary holds to the contrary."

"And now you, the President, will not let us work. You will not let us participate in society. We are shunned. But, despite your shunning, you will not let us leave!"

"This must now end! I am just a student. I am not an orator. I have never been involved in politics. I am no leader of my people. But if no one else will come forward and give this message, I will! And the message is, "Let my people go!"

In the video Ari closed his eyes as if deep in thought. He was clearly trying to control his emotions.

Opening his eyes, he repeated, "Let my people go! You must open the borders of the U.S. and let the Jews depart." He paused. "This is the right thing to do. It is the humane thing to do. It is the only thing to do. You cannot keep us here, within, but isolated from, society! You cannot do this! It is intolerable!"

Ari paused again.

"But I do not simply ask you to let us leave. I demand that you do this!"

"If you do not heed my words, I will call down a plague upon this country. And not just one plague! But enough plagues so that, hard-hearted like Pharaoh you may be, in the end - like Pharaoh - you will let my people go!"

Again he paused.

"But you do not need to suffer any of these plagues. If by June 10th, seven days from now, you announce that you will let the Jews of America depart, I will not send the plagues."

"But if you fail to do so, the first plague shall come – and it will not be locusts or boils!"

Ari then told the President what the first plague would be. It was the first of the three plagues he and I had discussed at that last dinner in our apartment!

Ari turned and pointed to the flag on the wall behind him.

"Heed my words!" he shouted. "We love this country! We do not do this thing lightly! Let my people go!"

Then the video ended.

In the darkened room on the old estate, even the battle-toughened Mossad agents were moved. No one spoke.

No one had expected anything like this.

I knew what I must do, of course.

Ari had signaled me to create the first plague if the President did not open the gates by June 10th. I had to get to work.

46

Ari's video went viral. It was watched by millions of people.

Spontaneous demonstrations erupted across the country.

Opinion leaders from every part of society called on the President to release Ari Cohen and his friends and to open the borders to the Jews.

T-shirts with Ari's face and the slogan "Let My People Go!" were everywhere.

The media rushed to publish pop-biographies of Ari and his family.

Ari was quickly dubbed "the American Moses."

It was as if Ari's video had given the American people a way to vent all their frustration and anger - not just at Part Two but at all the oppressive actions of the Administration.

There were counter-demonstrations, of course, by supporters of Part Two and closed borders.

The attack dogs of the Left and of the Islamic front groups, like MAFR, denounced Ari's video as a pathetic fraud. They demanded that the President not give in.

"Why would a President of the United States ever surrender to so patently specious a "demand" from a Jewish criminal?" said MAFR in a press release. "Cohen is an admitted criminal. He confesses he aided Jews to sneak out! He should be executed - as an example to other Jews who might consider such things!"

For three days following the video there was no response from the Administration.

During those three days the public outcry and the Left-Islamic response grew in geometric intensity.

Over one hundred million people had now seen Ari's video. The Administration had to do something.

Finally, on the fourth day, the President issued a statement. It said:

"Ordinarily the President of the United States would not respond to a pop-video from a self-inflated criminal who, claiming that he or his friends have been arrested by this government, makes insane demands on behalf of an entire group of people, most of whom do not even know who he is."

"However, because of the disruption created by this criminal - and out of concerns for public safety and good order - the President feels it necessary to respond."

"The President's response is very simple. This criminal's demand is nothing more than a terrorist threat. The United States does not negotiate with terrorists."

The President's statement continued: "To repeat, we do not negotiate with terrorists. We do not surrender to threats. The demands of this criminal are not just illegal. They would delegitimize the lawful structure of the Temporary Agent of Oppression Regulations - indeed, the Victims Law itself."

"Agreeing to these demands would be to confess that our entire system of social justice is fraudulent - which it most certainly is not!"

"We have the most enlightened, the most just legal structure in the world - which we have been able to craft only through the hard work of Democratic administrations since 2008. We will not surrender our just society to anyone, much less a benighted criminal in a You-Tube video! Therefore we reject these illegal demands! We reject them utterly! And that will be the end to this matter!"

After the President's response, there was no point in waiting until June 10th for the first plague. It had to be now.

I discussed this with Menachem. He thought for a bit, then said that we must have a conference with Uri and Rachel immediately.

A few minutes later we were looking at Uri and Rachel on video screens.

I told them all what the first plague would be. It was the plague that Ari had described in his video. I said it was the first of the three plagues I had outlined to Ari at our last dinner.

"If he has two more plagues, then he must have two more videos," said Rachel, jumping several steps ahead. "He must have planned for the President's rejection. Just like Pharaoh. And two more to come."

"It took ten plagues to persuade Pharaoh," said Uri.

"This President is no Pharaoh," said Rachel.

"I hope you are right," I said. "Because I have only three plagues."

"You could do more if you have to," said Rachel. "But three should do it." She was typically brusque and to the point.

The Mossad techs figured out that Ari's video had been released from Denver, Colorado. They asked why Ari would pick Denver.

I remembered Ari mentioning his night with Rabbi Naomi Goldman. I had sensed at the time that Ari felt something special about that relationship. I told Mossad that Ari must have made the videos and given them to Naomi to release if anything happened to him.

"Rabbi Naomi is in great danger," said Menachem. He put another call through to Rachel. After a brief discussion in Hebrew, he turned to me and said, "We must try to warn her. Unless she or Ari knew how to send an encrypted video, the feds will track her down. We must get to her and save the other two videos."

On the screen Uri turned back to Rachel and spoke again in Hebrew. At the end both nodded in agreement and the screen went dark.

"We will send a team immediately to pick her up," said Menachem. "Let us just hope we are in time."

Meanwhile there was still no word of Sarah or Stavisky.

Nor had either tried to contact me.

This was strange. Even though we knew it would be risky to call or email if we were being hunted, we had planned two or three short coded messages for such a case.

However, now there was just silence.

I tried not to let my fear for Sarah affect my concentration, but it was hard.

I focused on the first plague. The idea for it had come from the plague virus that I developed while working with Stavisky.

The concept was simple - to burn and destroy the hard drives of the personal computers, and also the email accounts, of all Democrats in Congress - as well as all members of the President's cabinet, the head of each federal administrative agency, and the leaders of the Democratic National Committee. And to make it look like the work of the NSA!

In his video Ari told the President that the first plague would destroy the computers of important people; but he had not said how. Nor did he say that the destruction would come from the NSA.

Converting my plague virus for such a task, and then sending it to personal emails through the NSA system, was easier said than done.

First we had to find the names of all the targets. The Mossad techs helped to do that. Altogether there were almost 700.

I then had to get inside the NSA files, find each name, and dispatch the plague virus to every recipient.

Since I still had my "back-door" key to the NSA files, getting inside was easy. The next step was then to apply my cloaking program to make my trespass invisible.

Finding each one of 700 email addresses could have taken days if I had not worked out a special program for this purpose. That special program combined finding the target email with sending the plague virus.

After I entered the Mossad list of target names into the program, the program searched the NSA Victim files, found the "official" personal email of each target, then dispatched the plague virus to that email.

The "official" email was the legal email address that each American was required to file with the NSA when registering under the Victims Law to obtain his or her V-Cert. To change it needed a formal notification process that most Americans would dread.

No one, even Victims of the highest categories, wanted much contact with the government. Thus very few people elected to change their "official" emails after the initial V-Law registration.

For this reason I guessed that the official NSA emails would key into the personal computers of the targets.

Even with my special programs, and with the Mossad list of 700 names, sending the first plague to all recipients took several hours.

The effects were immediate, however, and the outcry huge!

Word leaked instantly to the media, of course.

It would have been impossible to cover up the complete destruction of the personal computers and email files of more than 700 prominent people!

The plague was more destructive than even I could have expected.

After penetrating the entrails of the target's computer, like an infectious bacteria it divided and subdivided, destroying not only the hard drive but also penetrating all email addresses saved in the hard drive - and then destroying the hard drives of all persons who had received emails from the target within the last seven days!

The exponential effect was huge.

I was thankful the virus did not go beyond this second tier of email addresses - thankful because I did not want to do widespread damage, merely to terrify the first- round targets.

Why the first plague 'ran out of gas' after the first round I did not know (until later, when I had quiet time to figure out the answer). In any event, it was enough for its purpose. It affected almost 3,000 people! Dayenu! Enough!

The headlines followed immediately. All mentioned Ari Cohen.

"Moses Sends First Plague!" "Moses' First Plague Hits Dem Computers!" "Computer Plague Hits Democrat Leaders!" "First Plague Hits - What Now, White House?" The plague virus was the lead story in every newspaper and TV news program.

Some leading Democrats who had previously resisted "blackmail by a fraudulent Moses" now called on the President to let the Jews go.

"Let them leave!" said the Senate Majority Leader. "Why keep them here? The Justice Department documented their criminal history. Why, if the historical record is so clear, should we keep them in this country - but outside society? It's crazy! And it is not worth risking any more plagues! Who knows what the next will be?"

Hard-core Leftists and Islamists opposed this view. The first plague only hardened their resolve.

In yet-another press release MAFR called for tightening of Part Two rules to further restrict Jews from living any semblance of a normal life. "They must be punished for this plague!" said the MAFR release. "They must be taught that the President of the United States does not back down to puny threats of Zionist pigs!"

There was also a huge outcry as to how the NSA could have been used to send the first plague. How could Ari Cohen, a student, orchestrate such devastation through the NSA's own systems?

Committees of both House and the Senate scheduled hearings. The President demanded accountability from the National Security Advisor, the FBI, and the CIA.

Opponents of the TAgOp Regs said the NSA's involvement showed the unintended consequences of a police state out of control.

Tragically, the day after the first plague, Mossad learned that DHS had arrested Rabbi Naomi Goldman. They raided her synagogue only hours before a Mossad rescue team arrived.

The synagogue was cordoned off as a crime scene. Mossad reported that DHS brown shirts were posted inside and around the building. Where they took Rabbi Naomi Mossad did yet not know.

The White House immediately announced a breakthrough in what they called the "Moses Plot".

The White House Press Secretary said that a co-conspirator of the criminal Ari Cohen, the woman rabbi Naomi Goldman, had been arrested in Denver. The Press Secretary said Rabbi Goldman had confessed at once to being complicit in the plot and releasing the YouTube Video.

"Effective law enforcement by DHS has brought to an end this pathetic attempt to coerce the President of the United States," said the Press Secretary. "There will be no more of this wretched blackmail."

So much, we thought, for Ari's attempt to be the American Moses.

We were wrong.

47

The next day Ari's second video appeared on YouTube.

Ari appeared, as before, in the white room with the American flag on the wall. He wore the same white clothes and kippah. He was, if anything, sterner and more serious than in the first video.

While he may have made the second video shortly after the first, the emotion of what he was doing seemed to have aged him, even in so short a span.

"This is a second message to the President of the United States," Ari said.

"If you, the President, are viewing this, you have disregarded my first warning. You have suffered the devastation of the first plague. You - you yourself - have brought unnecessary harm to many people. And you have not agreed to let the Jews of America depart."

"This is a terrible thing you have done. And it is not just the Jews. What you are doing to the Jews is, of course, unconscionable. But you are rending apart the rest of American society - this wonderful America which was a beacon to the world."

"How could you not consider that you are destroying - indeed, have destroyed - the America which all of us, Jews and non-Jews, have so loved and have worked so hard to create?"

Ari could not stop himself from sobbing. "But we cannot go backward. We cannot put together what has been riven apart. All I can do is to repeat my demand that you let my people go!"

"Let my people go! Let my people go! If you do not do this - if you remain obdurate, if the forces of evil continue to harden your heart, there will come a second plague."

Ari then described what the second plague would be. As before, he set a deadline - seven days from the date when this video was delivered.

The camera then zoomed in for a close-up of his face. "You may or may not see my face again. I do not know what will happen to me. But to my fellow Jews - and to the good people of America, I ask you to remember the words of Moses' parting sermon to his people - to which we have hearkened so often in times of trouble."

Ari then repeated the words of Moses, scanning a few times at a small piece of paper:

"See -I have placed before you today life and good, and death and evil - that which I command you this day, to love the Lord your God, to walk in His ways, to observe His commandments, His decrees, and His ordinances. Then you will live and multiply, and the Lord your God will bless you....But if your heart turns away and you do not listen, and if you are led into the worship of other gods...I tell you today you will surely be lost....I call heaven and earth today to bear witness - I have placed before you life and death - the blessing and the curse. Therefore choose life, that you will live!"[‡‡‡]

At the end he lowered the piece of paper and looked directly at the screen. "Therefore choose life!" he said.

The screen went dark.

Once again, in the darkened room on the old estate, no one spoke.

[‡‡‡] Deuteronomy, 30 edited translation.

48

Not surprisingly, Ari's second video was more viral than the first - viewed this time by <u>hundreds</u> of millions of people.

As before, pro-Ari Cohen demonstrations erupted spontaneously in cities large and small. Americans of all backgrounds called on the President to let the Jews leave.

There were also, as before, huge counter-demonstrations. The Left and their Islamist allies did not sit quietly in the face of such a threat to their ideologies.

People fought each other in the streets. Local law enforcement was overwhelmed.

The turmoil was so great the Administration waited several days for it to subside. It did not.

It was as if Ari's second video had opened a door long locked in American society.

A very large majority of Americans realized now how fed up they were with years of government over-regulation, of government dictating the do's and don't's of their daily lives.

It was not just rigid strictures like the Victims Law, which told them who could attend schools or get jobs. It was not just the outrageous TAgOp rules.

It was the entire politically correct nanny state - governing how much fat they could eat and what they could do with small creeks in their back yards, what size child-seats they must put in their cars and what textbooks their children must read in school, why civil rights permitted violent criminals to shoot up large cities while little boys could not play with toy pistols, why OSHA imposed impossible-to-comply-with workplace rules but public schools could not fire criminally-miscreant teachers. The list of average Americans' grievances was endless.

Average Americans were fed up. But what power did they have? Their only recourse was to demonstrate in the streets.

Again the President could not remain silent.

In a statement condemning Ari Cohen, the President re-stated that this Administration would not negotiate with terrorists. The President promised, also, that DHS, the FBI, the CIA, and the NSA would not allow another plague.

"We will block this Ari Cohen and his criminal cabal from any more destruction. Be assured we are taking steps to stop Cohen's threatened next plague - or any other plague - from ever harming the people of the United States. We know who is doing this."

The last sentence of the President's statement was a lightning bolt to our small team in the secluded South Shore estate.

"They know where we are - or think they do!" said Menachem. We were speaking with Uri and Rachel in a hastily-called video conference.

"Go to Plan 2!" said Rachel. "Immediately!"

Plan 2 meant a repeat, in large scale, of what I had done in my apartment, only this time on the South Shore estate. It meant destroying all computers and other tech we could not quickly dismantle and take with us - and packing everything else for flight.

Plan 2 meant, also, doing quick searches of federal computers and databases for any sign they had found us.

As before, using Mossad's lightning-fast search techniques, we found no sign that the NSA or any other agency had knowledge of our existence. But we could be wrong.

If I could develop a cloaking program, why could someone else not do the same? It was tempting to assume we were right, that they did not know about us.

But we could not take a chance.

So in two hours Mossad packed up its super-secret hardware and destroyed what remained. They then cleaned the estate to leave no trace that we had been there; and the team split up in small groups to depart.

I was sad to leave the estate and to see the team disperse. I had been there only a short time but had become fond of the place and the team.

Most of the team left in non-descript vans and cars like the blue van that had picked me up. Menachem and I, with two of the tech team, had different transport, however.

Inside one of the barns was something I had not seen before - a stealth helicopter. When they wheeled it from the barn, I thought I was in a sci-fi movie. It was the most amazing helicopter I had ever seen - a thing of subtle dark surfaces and strange angles, to say nothing of an engine and rotors that made no noise whatsoever.

"If you see this from more than 50 feet, you see only a computer-generated image of the area around the bird," said Menachem. "It adapts to surroundings like a chameleon. If there is a tree behind it, or a cloud, you see only the tree or the cloud. Now get in."

We took seats in the strange bird and buckled in. Then, without a sound, we were off.

From inside we could see everything around us. It was, Menachem explained, a different version of the outside system. It allowed us, from the inside, to see everything visible from the outside, as if we were looking through huge picture windows.

As we climbed and headed north, not even two miles from the estate, we saw a line of black SUVs headed for the estate.

The President had not been bluffing! They had found our safe house!

Now we had to figure out how they found us!

As we watched, the black SUVs stopped the one Mossad van that was headed in their direction. Brown-shirts surrounded the van and forced the two Mossad agents inside to come out with their hands up. The brown-shirts then handcuffed the agents, pulled black hoods over their heads, and pushed them into one of the SUVs.

In the invisible helo our team said nothing, but their mental curses were loud. "It's Chaim and Dov," said the pilot. There was grim silence.

We could do nothing but fly on.

While the helo continued north along the coast, I worried about my beautiful Sarah. Strangely, I kept thinking of her naked with the Six Green Harmony around her neck. Where was she?

When I discussed this with Menachem, he told me to be hopeful. "If they had arrested her, don't you think they would have announced it? She is a much bigger prize than poor Rabbi Naomi!"

Menachem was probably right. It was the thinnest strand of hope, however.

Between continuing thoughts of Sarah, Ari, and Stavisky (where was Stavisky?), I started work on the second plague.

I did not know how much time I had left. If DHS located our Mossad safe house, they might have done so by tracking my NSA hacks.

If DHS could track my NSA hacks, they knew who I was (at least in cyber signature). They might be able to track my whereabouts. Also, they might be waiting for my next attack and might be able to block the second plague.

In such event Ari's courageous videos would have been for nothing.

It then occurred to me that the feds might <u>not</u> have Ari!

If they did, would they not have paraded him before the cameras? Would they not have wished publicly to humiliate him, to denigrate him?

Yet if the feds did not have Ari, where could he be? Was he, indeed, the one member of our Second Team who had escaped?

But where was he - and why had he not tried to contact me?

With so many questions clouding my brain, even as I watched the coastline below, I thought about the conceptual structure of the second plague.

Unlike the first plague, when I could use the already-created plague virus, this time I had to start from scratch. I did not need to use the NSA files, however, because I had all the data of the 700 targets from before.

The task was far more complex, however, because, in his second video, Ari had described the nature of the second plague in some detail. Hence I knew that the feds and the banks would be taking every possible step to thwart me.

The concept was simple. I would freeze the personal bank accounts of the same 700 targets whose computers I had fried in the first plague.

I would limit the damage to those 700 because I did not want to cause harm to ordinary Americans.

I had outlined this second plague to Ari that same night when he came to dinner. Obviously he had made careful mental notes of that conversation. What we had not discussed was how much time I needed to craft this plague - if I could do it at all.

There were several steps involved.

First, I needed the personal email addresses of the target group. This step was completed because I had already obtained those addresses for the first plague and had saved them in two separate but duplicate files.

Second, using those addresses as a starting point, I had to locate one or more bank accounts for each target.

Third, I had to hack into each bank account.

Fourth, I had to freeze each account, meaning no withdrawals and no deposits for an indefinite term. And, of course, I had to be invisible.

This would be, as you can see, no walk in the park. And, to make Ari's threat credible, I had to craft and execute this hack in two or three days.

While I would be "starting from scratch", I already had two core elements of this hack in addition to the address of each target.

In my junior-year bank hack at Stuyvesant I had learned the protocols to penetrate most bank security systems - which I hoped had not changed much since then. And, of course, I had the cloaking program.

I also had a handicap I did not have before.

Because Ari had already given warning, as I said, the banks and the targets knew I would be coming. Even now their best brains would be creating defenses to stop me.

So I would need a new weapon to counter their counters.

And, of course, they would try to track me back to the source of my attack.

Watching the coastline pass beneath the helo, I wondered about the effectiveness of my NSA cloaking program. Had the NSA been watching me all along? Instead of me being the cat and they the mice, had I been the mouse?

Yet why would they have played such a game - why allow me to change files to convert Jews to non-Jews? Why allow me complete freedom to roam their files?

If this were true, moreover, who was the brain opposing me on the other side of this elaborate chessboard?

Whatever my personal talents and achievements, I was never so vain as to think there were not smarter people in the world. There were always smarter people - just as there were always better-looking or richer people. That was the human race. But whoever this was, he or she must be very smart indeed.

A stunning thought hit me.

Could the NSA have known from the outset what I was doing? Could they have known every detail of our efforts to liberate departees?

This idea was so absurd it could not possibly be true. Yet what if it were true? For months we had operated openly and without any hint of someone watching. The key question would then be <u>why</u>?

49

The helo suddenly banked to the right and headed out to sea.

Perhaps two miles out we landed on the rear deck of a non-descript coastal tanker. It looked like every other rusty ship you might see plodding the waters of the Northeast.

Inside, of course, were not the dingy rooms of an old tanker.

It was almost a different planet – a 21st Century high-tech Mossad listening station. The technology in the old South Shore estate had been first class but temporary. Here, however, was a wizard-like complex you might only see in movies. I thought I had seen every kind of computer set-up; yet even I was awestruck.

The living quarters were Spartan but comfortable. I was given a two-person bunkroom for myself and told to get some sleep.

I told Menachem that I had to keep working on the second plague. "It will wait," he said, joking. "No plague was ever late to the office! You absolutely must rest - at least, take a one-hour nap. Then you can resume your magic."

I set my watch alarm for an hour and crashed on the lower bunk. The alarm did not wake me. After what seemed like ten minutes but was more than two hours, I felt a tug on my shoulder. It was one of the woman techs who had come with us in the helo. "Rachel wants to speak with you," she said.

I threw some water on my face and then dried with a towel. In the small mirror over the sink I saw a haggard, unshaven man I almost did not recognize. How long had it been since I slept through the night?

Rachel was not on the ship, of course. Instead, she was waiting for me from a large screen in one of what I thought of as the 'galactic' rooms.

"You look like hell," she said. Then, without pausing, she said, "We think we found your Sarah."

I must have looked crazed.

"We think she is O.K," said Rachel. "We think she is in her parents' brownstone in the West Village."

Her parents' house! It was the one asset they did not have time to sell before they departed. Sarah must have gone there in desperation because there was nowhere else to go. But why hadn't she tried to contact me?

"She probably was afraid any email or call would disclose her whereabouts or lead DHS to you," said Rachel, as if reading my mind.

"Can you get her?" I asked. "Can you get her away? If the feds know who she is, they will check her parents' house!"

"We are trying," said Rachel. "We are trying. After what just happened at the estate, we have to be doubly cautious."

Rachel gave me a fixed stare. "We don't know how they found us. They may even know you – and/or we - are out here! We don't want to jeopardize Sarah or this ship. So we will move carefully. Meanwhile you must execute the second plague. And quickly, before they find us again."

It was a typical to-the-point Rachel conversation.

So I started work with an expanded group of Mossad techs on the old tanker, and with some of the best computer tools in the world.

One of the techs, Jacob Gold, identified himself as the Mossad team leader who had been trying to keep up with me on my forays into the NSA files. Jacob said they had figured out how to piggyback on my early hacks but had been left behind by my cloaking program.

"That is a masterpiece," he said, with no trace of an Israeli accent. "When we finish here, when we are all done, you must show me how you did it."

Jacob was not your typical computer geek. In fact, with close-cropped beard, a jagged scar on his left cheek, and a muscular frame, he looked more like a Navy Seal. I asked what he did before joining Mossad. "I was a U.S. Navy Seal," he said.

Good for that, I thought. Who better to have your back, even in computer warfare?

I now worked to patch together the different parts of the second plague. With the help of Jacob and his team, this took less time than I expected - about 24 hours all in. The day after landing on the tanker I was ready to hit the trigger.

We were standing in the main galactic room of the ship, Jacob, his team, and I. 'Nothing ventured, nothing gained," I said.

"Fortune favors the bold," said Jacob, adding another appropriate cliché.

I wondered what joke Ari would have made. All I could think of was the Rabbi's mice.

I hit the key to launch the second plague.

No one said anything.

Instead we watched the progress of the plague on the large-screen monitors. In flashing yellow and green lights the monitors showed how the plague spread into and then out from the email addresses of the 700 targets to their banks. Then we followed the lights and the scrolling pages of code as, in every bank, the plague froze the targets' accounts.

In a matter of minutes, as we watched, the second plague brought personal financial havoc to the leaders of the Administration, to all Democrats in Congress, and to the heads of federal agencies.

The primary effect was to freeze each account. Because I had used a special encryption code, it would take days, if not weeks, for all the accounts to be unfrozen.

The secondary effect was to block scheduled payments from those accounts to payees who were to receive the payments. All automatic payments would now fail. This would lead to a daisy-chain effect of non-payment and default notices.

As in the case of the first plague, the secondary effect was widespread and devastating.

The outcry from the targets was immediate and, if anything, more pained than after the first plague.

But this time fear mixed with outrage. Democrat Senators and Congressmen now demanded that the President let the Jews leave.

"Who cares about them?" asked one Senator. "Why do we keep them if we think they are criminals? Why should we suffer these terrible plagues to keep people we don't want anyway?"

Others, shocked, called out the incompetence of the Administration.

"How can you not stop this?" asked a Democrat Congressman from Michigan. "They told you it was coming! What kind of computer idiots do you have? What kind of national security do we have? This is insane! I demand that Congress have emergency hearings to determine how this could happen!"

The media and the blogs echoed these refrains.

Republicans - and all who opposed the TAgOp rules, of course - clamored for the President to let the Jews leave.

If Congress had no power of repeal, if they were powerless before an Imperial Presidency, they could still speak out

"For the love of God, let them leave," said a Republican Senator from Texas. "Even if we are now an Apartheid country, at least we can let these people leave. If they can patch together a better life elsewhere - and who knows what futures they will have - justice and morality dictate that they must be allowed to leave!"

As with the first plague, the President initially delayed public comment on the second plague.

Two days passed, while the country held its collective breath, waiting for another video from Ari or a statement or action from the White House.

I was now frantic about Sarah. The Mossad team sent to find her had found only an empty house! Where was she, and why could I not reach her?

At that point events exploded in ways no one could have expected.

50

While Americans - and, indeed, many other countries - debated the future of U.S. Jews, Canada and Mexico both passed legislation granting asylum to any American Jews who could cross their borders.

The legislation which Canada's P.M. had proposed earlier passed with large majorities in both houses of the Canadian Parliament. This legislation was something American Jews had been watching for months.

Mexico was the big surprise. With a small Jewish population, Mexico was not known as being particularly hospitable to Jews. Nonetheless, media reported that the President of Mexico had been in contact with the Canadian Prime Minister and had then pushed through the legislation to let Jews into his country.

My Mossad friends, always cynical, thought both countries saw a huge opportunity if they could absorb U.S. Jews. "Why would they not?" asked Menachem. "Where else could you find - wholesale - such an amazing group of educated, hard-working, and civilized people?"

"Even if crazy," I said.

"Even if crazy," said Menachem. "Why not take a bunch of crazy potential Nobel laureates? Not much - as you say - 'downside'".

Not much downside indeed. "Except for the lawyers," I joked.

"Perhaps they will reconsider taking the lawyers," said Menachem.

The announcements from Canada and Mexico added frenzy to the U.S. debate - but did something more. They galvanized the entire American Jewish community.

Where before there was despair, now there was possibility. Nothing had been worse than being imprisoned in the U.S. as third-class - or, indeed, non-class - citizens. While none wanted to uproot themselves, American Jews now had true choices for a civilized future - if they could only get across a border.

Just as important, the announcements from Canada and Mexico opened a door to Israel.

Not surprisingly, Israel was the first destination of choice for many American Jews - but they could not get there if they could not cross the border. Now, if they could get to Canada or Mexico, they could get to Israel!

There had been strident opposition in both Canada and Mexico, of course.

A vocal minority in each country, mainly the Left and the Islamists, argued that all Jews were complicit with the Zionist war criminals of Israel and should not be allowed in. (Indeed, the same groups argued that Jews should also be expelled from their respective countries.) Other groups simply did not want an influx of refugees with who-knew-what consequences.

Yet in both Canada and Mexico the majorities in favor were large for many reasons - and not just humanitarian. There was a definite view of 'sticking it' to the U.S. after so many years of American hauteur.

The White House and the State Department were furious, of course. Having its two great neighbors open their doors to U.S. Jews was a rebuke of great dimension.

However, in what appeared to be one of the few wise decisions of this Administration, the President said nothing. The matter was reaching crisis dimensions. To add an international furor would only complicate and distract.

Then, however, the White House did something really stupid.

It released a still photo of Ari Cohen's dead body.

51

Ari was dressed in the same white clothing and kippah that he had worn in the videos. His body was seen lying in a street outside what appeared to be a prison-like building. There was a large bloodstain across his chest.

The White House statement accompanying the photo said the "AgOp traitor Cohen" had been shot while trying to escape DHS custody.

"The traitor Cohen had just been arrested and was being transported to court for arraignment. He had been read his rights and, like every citizen, would be allowed representation by legal counsel and due process of law. Instead he chose to resist. He grabbed a pistol from one of the officers escorting him, shot the officer, and attempted to flee. Another officer escorting him had no choice but to shoot."

"These events are tragic - but all who see this picture be warned! The United States will not tolerate extralegal challenges to its duly enacted laws. The President hopes the traitor Cohen's death will bring an end to foolish challenges to the TAgOp Regs."

The White House gave no details as to how Ari had been arrested or why the non-violent Ari would try to grab an agent's gun and shoot him.

The news of Ari's death stopped the world.

Even now, years later, people remember where they were and what they were doing when they heard the news - just as an earlier generation knew where they were when Kennedy was assassinated.

JFK's death had seemed to end the hope of a bright future where men could go to the stars and test limits of the possible.

Ari's death ended a more limited hope - that American Jews might escape this country, which had become their prison, to a better life elsewhere, however uncertain and perilous.

It was a crushing blow to those for whom Ari had been a shining light.

On that old tanker, rocking in a slow sea off the North Shore of Boston, there was silence. No one knew what to say. I was caught between grief and rage, unable to cry or to shout. One of the techs had frozen the image of the dead Ari on the screen. We stared at the lifeless form, paralyzed, unsure what to do.

"Turn it off!" I yelled. "For God's sake, turn it off!"

"I am so sorry," said Menachem. "As Jews we have all lost Ari Cohen - but I know he was your very good friend."

I just nodded, then turned and walked away to my cabin.

52

All across America there was grief and rage at Ari's death.

In temples and synagogues mourners recited the Kaddish. Non-Jews organized marches of silence in big cities and small towns.

The internet was afire, with thousands of postings of the White House photo of the dead Ari and millions of replays of Ari's two videos.

The opponents - the voices of the Left and the Islamists - dropped all pretense (if any ever existed) of legal justification for the TAgOp regime and persecution of the Jews. "This is a sign! This is a turning point! It is time for the camps!" said their websites. "Death to the Jews! Turn on the ovens! Let us now truly have the final solution!"

All Jews remembered Ari's last challenge to his people: "Therefore choose life!"

But Ari was no longer able to make that choice. Who would now come forth to speak for the Jewish people?

In the midst of my grief for Ari and desperation for Sarah I thought about the third plague I had discussed with Ari. I had no doubt I could execute it; but, without Ari to speak, what good would it do?

Three days passed.

Little work was done in America. Although people went to their offices and shops, phones did not ring and no one shopped, except for essentials. Production slowed in factories. The marches, the recitations of Kaddish, and the internet conflagration continued.

Then things began to unfold with a cascading effect.

First came a new video from Ari!

Ari was not dead!

It was the middle of the afternoon on the third day after the White House released the photo of the dead Ari. There was a loud banging on my cabin door. It was Jacob Gold, the Mossad-Navy Seal-tech. "Come quick!" he said. "You must see this!"

Together we raced to the tech room; and there on the screen, big as life, was Ari.

This time Ari appeared in blue jeans and a grey t-shirt, with a black kippah on his head. He was no longer in the white room. Instead he appeared to be on a hilltop or mountain lookout, with pine trees behind him.

Looking straight at the camera, he said simply, "My name is Ari Cohen, and I am not dead."

He turned around completely, pointing to the scene around him. "I am outside the United States," he said. "The photo you saw of my dead body was a fake! They photo-shopped my head onto someone else's body. To what vile depths will they descend to pursue their evil end?"

He held up the front page of a Canadian newspaper that showed the date as yesterday. So he had made this video yesterday! Thus it could not be a fake, for anyone who might try to claim otherwise.

Ari said that he knew he was being hunted but had decided to gamble. He said that the same genius who created the two plagues had changed Ari's DNA file in the government computers - so he was able simply to walk across the Canadian border, which he had done.

Obviously Ari had taken a chance that DHS would not expect him to hide in plain sight; but, with the blessing of the Lord, it had worked.

"This White House is evil and corrupt," he said, "but they are a bureaucracy - and they can be beaten." He shook his head defiantly. "They can be beaten!"

"You probably expect me to announce another plague," he said. "But I am not Moses, and the time for plagues is past!"

He looked intently at the camera. "Instead, we will take a lesson from another great man who also led his people to freedom -Mahatma Gandhi. Gandhi understood that unarmed people cannot use violence against a well-armed foe. So he made non-violence a political force. Now we will do so, too!"

Ari paused for emphasis. "The Jews of America will non-violently leave their homes and walk across the closest border. And no one will stop you!"

"I do not tell you that God has spoken to me," Ari said. "I do not tell you that this is divine inspiration. But I do tell you, from my heart of hearts, that this will work! It is a miracle that both Canada and Mexico have opened their doors. Now you must walk through those doors. Like the Israelites in Egypt, you must pack up quickly what you can, you and your children. You must make your way to the nearest border. And you must cross over!"

He paused again for emphasis. "You should go by car if you can - or by foot if you must. But you must go! You must go! And I tell you that, if you do this - if you all leave together in a massive departure - they will not stop you! They will threaten. They will try to frighten. But they will not stop you!"

Ari's voice was as strong and clear as it ever had been. "Prepare yourselves. Pack your belongings. Take what valuables you can take. Do what you must do to leave your homes forever. In three days you will depart. In three days you will travel with your families to the nearest border. You will cross over that border. You will non-violently cross over. And they will not stop you! They will not stop you! I say once again, "Choose life!""

The screen went black.

Two minutes later the screen lit up again, and Rachel's image appeared. "Where is he?" she asked, looking for me.

"Here I am," I said.

"Desist from the third plague!" she said. "Stop working on the third plague!'

Looking around the room, she said to the Mossad team, "Listen! Monitor! Watch! We believe the power of Ari Cohen will suffice! This is the turning point!"

Rachel shook her finger at us from the screen. "We will wait and watch. But you must watch carefully and be prepared! Even if they let the Jews out, they may be looking for you. They may still try to destroy your ship! Head further out to sea!"

The screen went dark again.

One thing puzzled me. "Where is Uri?" I asked Menachem.

He laughed. "You, who are so smart, haven't figured that out? Uri is the figurehead seen by the world. Rachel is the real head of Mossad!"

I was surprised, but not surprised. Mossad was layer upon layer of deception. With so many enemies of Israel, they had always to be five steps ahead of their foes.

I turned to help the Mossad techs with their surveillance programs. We would be the watchers to learn, if we could, what the U.S. government would or would not do to stop the Exodus from America.

All the prior events - the demonstrations, the internet clamor, the prayers, the shouts, the pain, the turmoil - were now as nothing.

Ari's video had launched the most viral flash-mob of all time. All over America, now, the Jews were preparing to leave. And their preparations were like a tearing up of great patches of earth, a rending of the life-fabric of America.

In big cities and little villages Jews began the tearful process of saying good-bye to friends and neighbors, of packing and throwing out, of fitting into one vehicle the distilled essence of their possessions and valuables.

It was much more than leaving homes, of course. It was a departure of the spirit.

In temples and shuls across the land rabbis and their congregants blessed Torah scrolls and put them carefully in boxes for the journey. Where next would these holy scrolls find permanent haven?

And Jewish families across the land carefully removed the mezuzot from the doorposts of their houses. Where next would they have doorposts on which to install the holy words?

Reacting to Ari's new video, the White House issued a terse statement. (The President did not appear in person or by video.) The statement said nothing about the photo of the "dead" Ari Cohen. The President demanded, instead, that the Jews ignore Ari's new video: "Jews of America, do not listen to the traitor Cohen! He says we will not stop you. But we will. We will stop you! Do not be fooled. We will use all legal means to stop you. We will even shoot if we must. No AgOp will pass over those borders!"

As if deaf to the White House statement, the Jews of America continued planning and packing.

Historians have long debated whether the Jews believed Ari's diktat that they would not be stopped, or whether they had simply reached their tipping point. Whatever the answer, they continued to pack and prepare, to ready themselves for whatever the future would hold. They were going to leave.

Then, on the morning of the third day, the Exodus began.

Families and children took last looks at their homes. They hugged and kissed the neighbors who had come to say good-bye (and who in many cases said they would look after their homes in case - you never know - the owners might someday return).

Someone sent the following quote, from William Bradford's Of Plymouth Plantation, to Hadassah AgOp, which she posted to a million viewers:

"At length, after much travell and these debates, all things were got ready and provided... A smale ship was bought, and fitted in Holand...So being ready to departe ...And the time being come that they must departe...they left that goodly and pleasant citie, which had been their resting place...but they knew they were pilgrimes, and looked not much on these things, but lift up their eyes to the heavens...The next day, the wind being faire, they went aborde, and their freinds with them, where truly doleful was the sight of that sade and mournful parting; to see what sighs and sobbs and prairs did sound amongst them, what tears did gush from every eye...But the tide (which stays for no man) calling them away that were thus loathe to depart...they tooke their leaves one of another, which proved to be the last leave to many of them..."

"Being thus passed the vast ocean...they had now no friends to welcome them...no houses much less towns to seek for succore...Besides, what could they see but a hideous and desolate wilderness, full of wild beasts and wild men...Neither could they, as it were, go to the top of Pisgah, to vew from this willderness a more goodly cuntrie to feed their hops..."[§§§]

After posting this quote, Hadassah AgOp wrote: "In how many other times, in how many other places, have Jews made similar departures, sometimes

---

[§§§] Original text quote from William Bradford, Of Plymouth Plantation, a Digital Edition, Early Americas Digital Archive, http://mith.umd.edu/eada/html/display.php?docs=bradford_history.xml

319

voluntary, sometimes forced? Yet this time it will be not hundreds, not even thousands, but millions. And where, next, will they find a goodly country to feed their hopes? That, alone, is why Israel exists!"

There had been some six million Jews in the United States. Most had decided now to leave. There was no future here. Even the most die-hard Jewish Democrats had to concede that the American dream was dead.

53

What looked, from the air, like vast caravans of cars and trucks began to snake along the roads of America towards the Canadian and Mexican borders. Waiting at those borders, and also at key points along the route, were lines of police and military vehicles massing to meet them.

Remarkably, even from the beginning, there was silence. It was deadly quiet.

And the police and military did nothing.

As the long lines of Jewish vehicles passed, there was no attempt to stop them; no shots were fired; no commands were given.

It was as if a divine command had been given, "No words".

At first the silence was just strange. Yet, as it persisted for mile after mile, as the Jews continued to pass along the roads, the silence grew upon itself, like some wordless anthem of a great movement.

Everyone - the passing Jews and the watching police and military - knew that something momentous was happening. So, too, did the huge crowds who were gathering to watch the Exodus.

The silence grew upon itself. All along the roads there was silence.

TV news reports all across the country showed video scenes without commentary. Everywhere there was silence. The Jews passed by; the police, the military, the crowds, the TV reporters were dead quiet. No one spoke. Everywhere there was silence.

It was, indeed, a wordless anthem. The wordless anthem became a thing unto itself, an unspoken cry of grief by and for all Americans, Jews and non-Jews, who knew what they had lost.

The Jews reached the borders and began to cross. No one stopped them.

For the next few days the Jews continued - in cars and trucks, RVs and buses, even motorcycles and bicycles - to stream along the roads and over the borders. No one said a word.

These came to be known as the "Days of Silence."

They were later celebrated annually in the American Diaspora by two days of fasting and remembrance

The White House was enraged, of course. The President convened an emergency meeting of the Attorney General and the Joint Chiefs of Staff.

"This is not possible!" said the President. "This cannot be tolerated! Where is obedience to the rule of law? Why haven't the army and the police stopped this?"

"This is not about the rule of law. The choice is between silence and shooting," said the Attorney General. "The American people will not accept shooting. Unfortunately this just evolved. And once it began, it could not be stopped."

"And therefore we must accept this, I see," said the President, "because the American people will not accept shooting. Is that correct?"

"They will not," repeated the Attorney General. "And the troops will not fire on them."

"Perhaps, indeed, they will not," said the President, standing up to conclude what had been a very short meeting.

One of the Joint Chiefs later wrote in his memoirs that it was as if the President were going through the motions to that point - as if the President had expected <u>and welcomed</u> the response because it gave him the excuse for what came next.

"So - now you know what you must do! Make the announcement!" said the President. There was silence in the Cabinet Room as the President departed.

One hour later the Justice Department issued this statement:

"Under the authority of Article I, Section 9 of the Constitution, effective as of 12:00 p.m. today, the President has declared, and hereby declares, martial law and has suspended the writ of habeas corpus."

"The   President has been forced to take such action by the Rebellion of those Americans who are classified as AgOps and who have resisted all efforts to require them to abide by the law."

"All citizens of the United States, and all agencies of government - federal, state, and local - will now take direction from the Executive Branch of the Federal Government until martial law is rescinded."

"As the first act of the President under martial law, the President has deemed it in the best interests of the United States to allow the wretched AgOps to depart. They have done enough to harm this great country. It is better now that they go and that the United States be rid of them."

"Accordingly, the President has ordered, and hereby orders, the Department of Homeland Security and all federal officials to permit the AgOps to cross the border unhindered."

"Given the great disruptions these AgOps have caused, the President had no other choice."

"The President believes this action to be in the best interest of the people of the United States. This declaration of martial law will be temporary. In due time, after the country recovers from the vast disruptions caused by the AgOps, the President will consider lifting this martial law. Thus, in time, the people of the United States of America can look to a better future, a future free of Agents of Oppression."

The President's declaration of martial law caused a furor, of course.

The fleeing Jews accelerated, if possible, their departure.

They flooded across the borders. All wished to be safe in Canada or Mexico before the President reversed position on letting them leave.

The rest of America was in shock. Americans did not know how to react.

We watched these unfolding events from the monitors in the 'galactic' room of the old ship, and from the emails streaming through our surveillance systems.

We were mindful, of course, that we might still be attacked. The President's release of the Jews did not mean that DHS or the NSA were not still looking for us.

We also continued hacking into government websites and emails to see if the President's announcement were a trick or a ploy. We found nothing to indicate that it was.

In the midst of all this I received two emails, one from Sarah, the other from Stavisky.

I opened Sarah's immediately. I did not have time to open Stavisky's.

Sarah was in Canada! Sarah was safe!

She had managed to cross the border two days before Ari's last video!

She said that, like Ari, she had simply driven across without incident. Since for security I had changed her DNA to non-Jew earlier, and since everyone thought she was Chinese anyway, there was no problem.

She had not contacted me before, she wrote, because she was in hiding.

She had been walking back to our apartment when she saw me being hustled into a van outside the building. Not knowing what to do, she stopped and watched from across the street.

She saw our van drive off, then had seen black SUVs descend on the building and DHS brown-shirts jump out and run into the building.

Putting two and two together, she immediately followed the escape plan we had agreed on weeks before.

She managed to catch a train to New York and then to get to her parents' brownstone. Then she did get my "18" message but was afraid to respond, by email or by phone. She could not know who might be listening or how.

After three days in New York, she began to worry that the brownstone was being watched. In desperation she took her parents' second car and drove to Canada.

She hoped, she wrote, that her email would reach me. She was desperate to let me know that she was safe - but she did not want to jeopardize me. She had to assume that any phone call or email would be watched and might lead them to me.

She knew, of course, that it was I who had launched the two plagues. She had no doubt about that! She would wait two days and then try again if I did not respond. "I love you and miss you so much!" she wrote.

I could feel the tears in her words. They mixed with the tears in my heart. But she was safe!

54

It was now the eighth day after the President had declared martial law and opened the borders.

Amazingly, almost all the Jews were now across - all those doctors and lawyers, teachers and accountants, dentists and actuaries, scientists, theater and film directors and producers, professors and librarians, musicians and actors, social workers and computer geeks, philanthropists and car dealers, real estate developers and investment bankers, small and large business owners, mothers and children - just ordinary men and women - all those whose only crime was to have Jewish DNA.

How would the loss of its Jews impact the United States? And what would be the impact on Canada, Mexico, and Israel of these new arrivals?

We had been working around the clock for all eight days, hacking into and monitoring federal communications while all this was happening. Now, exhausted, we slouched on couches in the common room of the old tanker.

What to do next? What would I do?

I would go to Canada and find Sarah - but then what? To Israel? To somewhere else?

Looking around the room, I had a question for my Mossad comrades.

"What was strange about all those federal emails we saw?" I asked.

No one answered.

"What was strange?" I repeated.

"I will tell you what was strange," I said. "In all those federal emails, in all those federal communications, there was no element of surprise or consternation after the declaration of martial law. It was just business as usual!"

I looked at the tough faces around the room. "Don't you think that was strange - just business as usual when the Constitution was abandoned?"

"Except for two things," said Menachem. "Two things are not business as usual." His words echoed in the small space:

"The Jews are free." He paused. "All other Americans are now prisoners of their own government."

EPILOGUE

I had forgotten about Stavisky's email. Don't ask why. The next day, when I did open it, I wished I had not.

Stavisky wrote:

"When you read this I will be dead."

"I cannot live with what I have done. I am getting old, anyway, and the world will not miss one decrepit Cossack-Jew. But I cannot make light of this. I only hope that by sending this message and enclosure to you I can do something, even if little, to make things right."

I noticed that Stavisky had included an attachment with his email. I waited to open it until I finished reading his message.

Stavisky continued: "I told you earlier about my daughter in L.A., the girl I had not seen in many years. Well (I thought, here, of him chewing on his pipe stem), they found her."

"The NSA found her. In those early days, when you first figured out how to convert Jews to non-Jews, before you created the cloaking program, they caught wind that we were up to something."

"At first they thought it was me. Don't ask me how they figured that out. Or maybe they just zeroed on me because I had Jewish DNA and knew the inside of their systems. Everybody knows they are institutionally paranoid!"

"Anyway, whatever the reason, they interrogated me. They arrested me and took me to that old building you found in downtown Boston."

"They really worked me over - but I did not break."

"I actually held out for several days. Then they found my daughter. They said they would take her and that she would never again see the light of day if I did not cooperate."

"It was either you, whom I loved like a son but who they were not going to grab yet because they wanted to find out what you were doing - or she, whom I barely knew anymore, who would be put away in a dark place - or worse."

"Even after this, I still held out. Then they seized her and showed her to me on a video screen, bound and gagged, terrified and ignorant, wondering what Hell she had fallen into."

"When she saw my face on the screen, she recognized me and vomited into her gag."

"I am a weak old man. I broke. I chose her instead of you. It was my 'Sophie's choice.'"

"From then on they knew everything you did - at least the part that I knew - and, of course, everything that I did. They followed all my meetings with the rabbis. And then they followed the Second Team."

"That is why it seemed as if no one was watching."

"I tried sometimes to give them disinformation. Sometimes it worked."

"Eventually I had to tell them about your cloaking program. But, since you never told me how you did it, I couldn't tell them! So they did not figure it out - and still can't to this day, even though they know you are doing it!"

"As I said, they followed all my visits to the rabbis, and Sarah's, too. And they knew about us sending off all our departees."

"But this is the really strange part. They didn't stop us! They did not stop us!"

"I began to wonder - why did they not shut us down? Why did they just watch and do nothing? What reason did they have to let us continue?"

"Then I decided to start watching my watchers. I guessed they would never expect me, their informant, to be watching them!"

"I could never repair the damage I was doing to you. But perhaps I might find some small thing as a gesture of atonement."

"So for days I watched and watched. I found nothing. Then, when I had just about given up, when I had decided that such tedious watching was no long worthwhile - I found the smoking gun!"

"The smoking gun is the document I attach to this email."

'What can be a smoking gun?" you may ask. "The answer - it is a secret memo from the Attorney General of the United States to the President of the United States!"

"How did I find it? Pure luck, just pure luck, because it was an <u>unsecured</u> "cc" to the National Security Advisor. How could something like this be unsecured? Why this email - of all possible secret, official emails - was not encrypted, I cannot guess. Some idiot just forgot to encrypt the cc!"

"Perhaps it was hubris of power or just typical government stupidity. In any event this memo will answer all your questions."

"They eventually did let my daughter go. She never tried to call me. She had to leave with the Exodus because she is now a Jew."

"Until her DNA swipe, of course, she did not know she was Jewish. That must have shocked her! She will, of course, never forgive me."

"Anyway, I waited until I knew she was in Canada to send this to you."

"You are the son I wish I had – and, of course, the most brilliant person I have ever known. (I can never forget that first day when you answered in eight minutes what no one else could do even halfway in thirty minutes!)"

"I hope and believe that you will continue this fight - you and Ari. While the Jews are safely out, while this one chapter has ended, I believe in my heart that there will be more, much more, for you and Ari to do to help your people - my people. Right now you may not understand this. But I think you will as time goes by."

I could barely continue reading.

"And now it is time to go," Stavisky wrote.

"I have some pills. It will be easy. I will simply go to sleep."

"I do not expect you to forgive me. I ask only that you try to understand. And never forget what you and Ari have achieved."

"This wretched memo that I enclose means nothing. You and Ari were the ones who did it. Whatever the vile ends of this President, it was you and Ari who gave the Jews of America a new life. They - and the world - will never forget."

The email ended.

I closed my eyes.

I prayed that Professor Pyotr Stavisky had gone gently to sleep and now, chewing a ghostly pipe stem, debated great ideas with his ancestors.

There was nothing left but to open the attachment.

It was a memo on the letterhead of the Attorney General of the United States - addressed to the President of the United States. The subject was "Operation End-Run."

It was dated the day after the release of Ari's last video. It read:

"To date we have vastly overestimated the reaction of American Jews and their allies to the TAgOp Regs. Not even Part Two, not even closing the borders, not even severe legal restrictions, caused the civil upheaval we had wanted and expected."

"They marched and petitioned. They filed lawsuits - but there was no rebellion! There was no violence! There was no insurrection! They did nothing to justify martial law!"

"That was your great plan - to make the Jews pariahs so as to cause a national explosion – which would then justify martial law. But nothing happened."

"The Jews and all the Jew-loving Americans were like sheep. They did not take up arms. They did not take to the barricades. They did nothing - except for the few who escaped with computer-changed DNA. They continued to obey the law!"

"This last Cohen video changes the paradigm. Now you win twice."

"Cohen's Exodus is the mass upheaval you wanted. Now, unquestionably, you can impose martial law."

"But you are now also magnanimous! You are the great and benevolent President who releases the wretched Jews."

"At one stroke, you take total control - and you are a wise and humane leader!"

I stopped reading.

It had all been part of a plan - the TAgOp Regs, Part Two, the border closings, everything.

It had all been part of a plan!

Ari was the catalyst they had needed all along - Ari and his videos and my plagues.

The Jews of America were not just victims, but pawns in a great chess game.

The whole thing, the entire TAgOp structure, was a mask for another purpose entirely.

I told the Mossad team. We were still on the ship, but had sailed north and were in now in Canadian waters.

They were not surprised.

"Evil is banal," said Rachel, matter-of-factly after she had seen the "Operation End-Run" memo. "These are the most wretched of so-called leaders. What leaders do this to their own citizenry?" she said. " Sadly, however, the American people surrendered long ago - when they allowed the passage of the Victims Law. Allowing the creation of an apartheid - and the Victims Law was an apartheid - no matter how well intentioned, had to end in tragedy."

But perhaps, I thought, this was not quite the end.

This was not quite the end.

In my anger at what they had done to Stavisky I had one last form of retaliation - the third plague.

I have a personal rule never to act immediately in anger. That day, after I had the idea that this was not the end, I followed my personal rule. I did not react immediately.

After reading Stavisky's message and the End-Run memo, I went out on deck for some sea air.

The sea was quiet, as it had been all the while we were on the old tanker. Based on the position of the sun, the ship was heading slowly north, rocking side-to-side in long, rolling swells.

339

I thought of the long chain of events that had brought me here.

How could I have guessed, when I hacked into Harvard, that within two short years I would meet and love Sarah and would help American Jews embark on a new diaspora?

Like those pilgrims embarking on the Mayflower, and then viewing a storm-tossed coast, I had no idea what the future held.

Like them, I could not "go to the top of Pisgah" to view from this wilderness a more goodly country to feed my hope.

But there was one thing I could do before I faced the future, and I now turned to the doing of it.

I went to the tech room and for the next six hours worked on the third plague.

I was not really starting from scratch, of course.

Beginning when I had discussed the third plague at that fated last meeting with Ari, I had worked out all the details in my head. Now it needed only execution.

I would use the cloaking program as a screen. Stavisky's email made clear that the NSA had not figured out the cloaking program.

They would soon enough find the effects of whatever I did. But the cloaking would blind them to the when and the how.

Menachem and Jacob came in to the tech room from time to time. They asked no questions but sometimes offered me coffee or a snack. They knew I needed to be left alone.

Getting into the NSA files was easy, of course. Nothing had changed. Use of the cloaking program prevented them from seeing me enter or roam through their data fields.

I was astonished that by now they had raised no better defenses.

Perhaps they assumed I would not return to their playing fields once the Jews had gone. What reason, after all, would I have to come back?

My only new task was to create what I called the "Devastator" program. "Devastator" was a good term, I thought, for what would be my contagion.

For this would truly be a contagion, an epidemic, a conflagration, a plague of plagues, all within the binary codes of the NSA file structures.

I worked with total intensity and focus on my task. I was "in the zone". Time stopped. There were only the codes on the screen and the math in my head.

Finally, after what seemed a short time but which in fact lasted eight hours, it was ready - the Devastator, the doomsday program.

I sat back in the chair and took a sip of cold coffee. Menachem had just entered the room.

"Still at it," he said. "We have not asked. We assumed you would tell us when you are ready."

"I'm ready," I said. "But do you think this needs a ceremony, or a solemn statement - or should I just push the button?"

We looked at each other.

"You know what?" I said, "To hell with it."

And I hit the 'enter' key.

For a moment nothing happened. Then it began, slowly at first, then faster, and faster and faster, and then of course at computer speed - the third plague.

The Devastator spread out like a nuclear fire into the NSA files and through all the Victims Law files. It was a nuclear fire.

Everywhere it coursed, it destroyed.

It destroyed the core programing of the Victim files.

It destroyed the data file on each and every Victim and non-Victim, and all the files on their ancestors and their DNA.

It destroyed all the pluses and minuses, all the management and internal files of the AO Directorate, everything.

It also burned the internal guts of every server that held any of these things. The Devastator was a nuclear fire.

In the end nothing remained of the vast administrative apparatus of the Victims Law.

There were no more categories or distinctions, no more advantages or disadvantages, between black and white, Latin and Asian, men and women, gender and gender, Jew and non-Jew.

All the Victims Law records - hundreds of millions of records, billions of records - were destroyed.

All servers were destroyed.

Everything was destroyed.

The Devastator was devastating.

I imagined a vast silence in the former computer realms of the NSA and the AO Directorate.

It would take months, if not years, to recreate even part of what was lost.

And as long as that took - if ever it could be done - all Americans would once more be equal before the law.

Hineni.

THE END

Josephus Publishing

Contact: josephuspublishing@outlook.com

Made in the USA
Lexington, KY
14 September 2015